"You've got it all wrong. I don't want to marry you—I don't even like you!"

There was a startled pause, during which Kat prayed for the ground to open up and swallow her.

"I have to tell you there are some serious flaws in your seduction technique, Miss Wray," Matt Devlin told her.

Kat's cheeks grew hotter as she squirmed under Matt's scrutiny....

KIM LAWRENCE lives on a farm in rural Anglesey, Wales. She runs two miles daily and finds this an excellent opportunity to unwind and seek inspiration for her writing! It also helps her keep up with her husband, two active sons and the various stray animals that have adopted them. Always a fanatical consumer of fiction, she is now equally enthusiastic about writing. She loves a happy ending!

> **Kim Lawrence's** fast-paced, sassy books
> are real page-turners. She creates characters
> you'll never forget, and sensual tension
> you won't be able to resist....

Books by Kim Lawrence

HARLEQUIN PRESENTS®
2123—HIS SECRETARY BRIDE (2-in-1)
2147—WIFE BY AGREEMENT
2161—THE SEDUCTION SCHEME
2171—A SEDUCTIVE REVENGE
2209—A CONVENIENT HUSBAND

Don't miss any of our special offers. Write to us at the following address for information on our newest releases.

Harlequin Reader Service
U.S.: 3010 Walden Ave., P.O. Box 1325, Buffalo, NY 14269
Canadian: P.O. Box 609, Fort Erie, Ont. L2A 5X3

Kim Lawrence

THE PROSPECTIVE WIFE

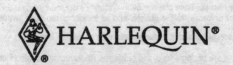

HARLEQUIN®

TORONTO • NEW YORK • LONDON
AMSTERDAM • PARIS • SYDNEY • HAMBURG
STOCKHOLM • ATHENS • TOKYO • MILAN • MADRID
PRAGUE • WARSAW • BUDAPEST • AUCKLAND

ISBN 0-373-12231-4

THE PROSPECTIVE WIFE

First North American Publication 2002.

Copyright © 2001 by Kim Lawrence.

Printed in U.S.A.

CHAPTER ONE

CAUGHT between a rock and a hard place the unfortunate orderly began to sweat. He'd met some real hard cases in his time, but this black-haired bloke, who even on crutches towered over him, could have given the hardest of those tough characters a run for their money! It was something about those eyes, he concluded with a shudder, as he became unable to maintain eye contact with those electric blue orbs any longer.

Truth to tell, he'd always felt slightly scornful of his colleagues, who tended to be intimidated by some of the rich and famous patients who stayed at the exclusive clinic. It was a matter of pride with him...no obsequious grovelling to the spoilt and pampered. He was polite, but he didn't treat them any differently than he would the ordinary man in the street. In his own defence there was no way this bloke was going to be mistaken for a man in the street, and that circumstance had nothing whatever to do with money.

'Sister said...' he began to protest weakly.

'Take the wheelchair away.'

No shouting, no red-faced blustering, but he still managed to put an indefinable *something* into his voice that made your blood run cold.

'Sister Nash said you've got to leave in a wheelchair.'

Matthew Devlin permitted himself a thin-lipped smile and remained blissfully unaware that the streetwise young man in front of him found it deeply sinister.

'Sister Nash knows my opinion of wheelchairs.'

The redoubtable Sister Nash knew Matt's opinion on a lot of subjects; they'd had many a clash of wills over the past few weeks.

5

'Listen, mate.' The harassed orderly made a last-ditch man-to-man appeal. 'Maybe you don't need the wheelchair, maybe you do; I don't know. I do know you won't be here tomorrow, but I will and so will Sister Nash. She can make life a misery.'

'Thanks, Martin. I'll see Mr Devlin off the premises.'

The orderly turned with an expression of relief to see Andrew Metcalf standing in the doorway.

'Cheers, Doc!' He gave him a grateful look and didn't hang around to find out if his appeal had found a sympathetic ear.

'Well, Matt, harassing my staff to the bitter end, I see...'

Matthew Devlin snorted. 'That's pretty rich, coming from you! If it's not beneath your dignity—' he nudged a slim leather briefcase with his toe '—carry that for me.' As much as he hated asking for help, sometimes there was no alternative.

The curt unfriendly tone didn't have any visible effect on the surgeon, who had a pretty shrewd idea of the frustration his patient was feeling.

'I doubt if it's on my job description but what the hell...for my favourite patient, why not?'

'Is sarcasm in the job description?' Matt gritted, swinging his crutches into action. Even though this posture robbed him of several inches, he was still a good head taller than the other man.

'You're in a hurry,' the doctor observed, increasing his pace to keep up with the cracking pace Matt had set. 'Anyone would think you didn't like us...'

'If I ever develop a yen to live in a police state you'll be the first person I think of, Doc,' Matt promised grimly.

'I suppose I'd be wasting my breath telling you not to discharge yourself...?' Matt delivered a look that could have withered grapes on the vine. The doctor gave a philosophical shrug. 'You can't blame me for trying. You are, after all, one of my most amazing success stories. I'd hate to see you blow all that hard work for the want of a bit of patience.'

Matt's smile was wintry. He'd made heavy inroads during the past few months into his limited patience reserves. 'Don't worry, I won't do anything to ruin your reputation as a miracle-worker.'

Andrew Metcalf inclined his head in acceptance of the back-handed compliment. His expression was wry; he knew he was good, possibly the best, but he was a realist, and as much as he would have liked to claim all the credit for himself he knew that the speed and completeness of Matt's recovery owed more to the man's remarkable determination and steely willpower than anything else.

'Back door to avoid the press…?' He knew the routine; the clinic had had its fair share of celebrity patients.

'I don't see why I should make their lives easier, do you? Joe's brought the car around.'

His doctor could see the reasoning behind this logic; he was pretty sure he might be a bit paranoid too if his personal life had been served up for public consumption as often as Matt Devlin's had.

'If you're so bothered about security I'm surprised you're not staying with your parents. Don't they even have their own drawbridge…?'

'Not to mention a moat, castle, and the best part of a village,' Matt drawled languidly. 'But no son… At least, not as far as my father's concerned.'

The doctor looked at his patient's perfectly proportioned, rather stern profile and wondered if he cared. You never could tell with Matt.

'But…' He stopped himself just in time from blurting out the information that Devlin senior, who had even more financial clout than his son, had forbidden any member of staff to mention. 'I'd have thought the accident…' he protested mildly.

'It would take more than a near-death experience to make

my father change his mind, Andrew. As far as he's concerned I stopped being his son the day I didn't do as he wanted. I'm the competition now...and he'd like nothing better than to ruin me.'

Andrew Metcalf was shocked by this cold-blooded analysis even though he knew it wasn't strictly true.

'Well, that's not likely to happen, is it?' he responded uncomfortably.

Despite the fact that after the somewhat mysterious departure of his more experienced partner the City had predicted disaster, it was well known that the airline Matt had started from very humble beginnings was now causing the big players who had scoffed—none louder than Matt's own father, Connor Devlin—serious headaches.

'Worried about your share dividend, Doc?'

Andrew grinned. He could afford to. Fair Flights was one of the financial success stories of the decade. 'Actually, I do have a small sum invested.'

'Then I'll probably make you a very rich man,' Matt announced with a total lack of modesty.

'The rates we charge here and the amount of hardware in that leg, Matt, you already have...'

'I've never actually done any private sector work, and to be honest it's never really appealed.'

Despite her indifferent tone Kat was well aware she couldn't afford to be picky when it came to jobs. In fact it was all she could do not to kiss the woman's hand-made Italian shoes!

Kat's anxiety began to mount as she watched Drusilla Devlin's china-blue eyes drift around the forlorn-looking, half-empty sitting-room. Supposing I sounded *too* uninterested? It was one thing not wanting to come over as a charity case; it was another playing hard to get!

'But you need work...?'

Kat felt a wave of relief. For a nasty moment there she'd thought she'd talked herself out a job.

'Don't we all?'

Well, not all, Kat silently conceded, realising that she was almost certainly speaking to someone who didn't need to work. The chauffeur-driven limo Drusilla had driven up in had been ample proof of that.

Kat's own situation wasn't *desperate,* but it could get that way...and fast. Her godfather was executor of her mother's estate and, even though he'd tried to break the news as gently as he could, Kat had been shocked to learn of the full extent of her mother's debts. Kat had genuinely thought the gambling thing was in the past.

Apparently she wasn't legally obliged to pay back the undocumented amounts of cash—some of them large—that her mother had borrowed from friends and family over a twelve-month period, but Kat was determined to pay back every penny!

It was a weight off her mind that the house had sold so swiftly; unfortunately this piece of good luck had left her without a roof over her head.

With very little in her bank account—the extended leave she'd taken to care for her mother during her final stages of her illness had been unpaid—she needed a job and somewhere to live.

Now here was a friend of Mum's who, up until last month, they hadn't seen for years, offering her both. It had to be fate!

She nudged the edge of a half-full packing case with the toe of her trainer. It was filled with the stuff the auctioneers hadn't wanted.

'People always want good physios, and I've heaps of experience. I'll get a new job easily enough,' she assured her affluent-looking visitor on an earnest, upbeat note.

'But not your old one.'

'No,' Kat confirmed with a regretful sigh. 'I knew they

couldn't hold it open indefinitely, but that might be a blessing in disguise.'

Drusilla wasn't surprised to hear it. Five minutes after she'd met Kathleen Wray she had realised that her old friend's daughter was as resiliently optimistic as she was beautiful. A few discreet enquiries into the girl's financial situation, added to what Amy had told her, had revealed she'd need every ounce of that youthful resilience.

'I've worked in the same hospital since I qualified—not exactly bold and adventurous.'

Drusilla wondered if Matthew would find the girl's smile as enchanting as she did. A frown tugged at her seamless brow as she contemplated her son's choice of female companionship.

'I always meant to travel,' Kat explained, her eyes shining with enthusiasm as visions of exotic sun-kissed shores rose tantalisingly before her eyes. 'I just never got around to it somehow...' The smile faded. 'There's nothing to keep me here any more.'

Drusilla caught up the young woman's hand in a comforting clasp. 'You did everything you could for Amy, my dear,' she insisted warmly. 'And you must take comfort from the fact that in the end she was here amongst all the familiar things that were dear to her, and with the daughter I know she loved very much.'

The motherly patting on the arm made Kat's wide-spaced grey eyes fill with tears—not that Drusilla Devlin, with her designer clothes, glossy hair and impossibly youthful face, was like any mother she knew.

'You're very kind. You say this job would only be short term...? It is a live in post...?' That would solve her immediate problem.

Drusilla clapped her prettily kept hands in delight. 'You'll do it for me? Excellent!'

'There is a job, isn't there? You're not just inventing one because you feel sorry for me...?' Her doubts emerged gruffly as she wiped a hint of moisture from the corner of her eye. 'Mum didn't ask you to watch out for me...?'

Drusilla laughed. 'Oh, there's a job all right; you'll *definitely* earn your money, my dear. Incidentally, you'll be working for me, not Matthew.'

Kat nodded. That was understandable. If the man had been in hospital for six months it was likely he didn't have the spare cash to pay for a private physiotherapist, and it was equally obvious his mother did.

'I suppose it will be some time before he'll be able to get back to work...I mean, pilots need to be very fit, don't they?'

'Pilots...?'

'You did say he was piloting a helicopter when he was injured?'

'Yes, that's right.'

Drusilla was looking a bit uncomfortable and Kat cursed her own insensitivity at referring to the accident.

'You'd probably be better off getting someone else,' she felt impelled to point out. 'You know I've specialised in working with children for several years now.'

'That might come in very handy when dealing with Matthew,' Matthew's mother reflected drily. 'At heart most men are little boys.'

Kat's fuzzy mental image of an over-indulged mummy's boy intensified.

'The problem is he's never had a day's illness in his life and he's not making the most *patient* patient, poor dear. He needs cheering up, and small wonder! That terrible accident was bad enough, but then that awful girl proceeded to dump him.' The blue eyes flashed with maternal ire. 'I suppose we ought to be grateful she waited for him to be taken off the critical list before she went ranting on hysterically to those awful newspapers about him never walking again! "Horribly disfigured," I ask you...!'

Kat's grey eyes softened with sympathy. 'I didn't

know... They can do marvellous things with facial recon-struction.'

'Heavens, no; there was hardly a mark on his face. Ob-viously you don't escape such a horrific accident with *no* scars,' Drusilla conceded. 'But the main problem was being forced to lie flat on his back with the spinal injury for so long; he's had far too much time to brood. I knew the moment I saw you that you were just the girl for the job!'

'Let's hope your son thinks the same.'

It seemed strange to Kat that her new patient wasn't hav-ing any say in the choice of his physio, but then for all she knew he might be the sort of man who let Mummy buy his socks for him!

There were a lot of men out there who still relied heavily on their mothers well into their thirties—she'd met one or two herself. She sometimes wondered if something about her screamed 'substitute mother'; they certainly seemed to gravitate towards her.

'Oh, I'm sure Matthew will love you.'

Nothing could have been more heartily confident than Drusilla's firm tone... So why was Kat getting the distinct impression things weren't quite as straightforward as the older woman was implying?

'He does know that you're...?'

'You might find Matthew a little...erm...resistant...' Drusilla was obviously choosing her words with care. 'But you must promise me one thing.' Her blue eyes gleamed with urgency as she caught hold of Kat's hand. 'Don't lis-ten to him if he tells you he doesn't need you. Promise me, Kathleen!'

Kat felt slightly uneasy and a little embarrassed by the older woman's intensity. 'You're the boss,' she agreed, a shade of unease in her voice.

Kat had appreciated that her mother's childhood friend had married money, but she hadn't appreciated how *much* money until she arrived at that lady's country *cottage*. A shooting box for some titled lord originally, its rooms were all on a grand scale and the opulent decor which was sympathetic to the period was out of this world. She just knew she'd live in constant fear of breaking some priceless ornament.

After the housekeeper—Kat's idea that her ill-defined duties might need to stretch as far as the kitchen and the odd bit of light housework were fast fading—had shown her to her room, where she'd found a large bouquet of flowers and a warm letter from Drusilla apologising for her absence, Kat had explored the neatly kept grounds.

She was repelling the over-friendly advances of a large bee which had detached itself from the low lavender hedge that ran the entire length of the neatly trimmed lawn when a gleaming black Jag drew up on the gravelled forecourt.

The opportunist bee took advantage of Kat's lapse in concentration and stung her on the inner part of her exposed forearm—great timing! She was vaguely aware that a good deal of door-slamming and gravel-crunching was going on whilst she was hopping around biting her lips stoically.

Kat was just getting on top of the pain when she heard a deep gravelly voice bad-temperedly demand, 'Well, don't just stand there, Joe, get rid of her!'

The strong clipped tones didn't fit with the firm image in her mind of a wan, pain-ravaged invalid. She opened her eyes and blinked back the tears of pain to find a tall gangly chap of about thirty looking anxiously down at her. He looked nice, but a picture of health.

'Are you all right?'

'I was stung by a bee.' She peered towards the area of her arm which was already puffy and inflamed.

'You poor thing. Let me have a look...'

So much for all the elaborate subterfuge to ensure his privacy! Someone at the hospital must have passed on the information to the press. Matt Devlin quickly got tired of waiting for Joe to get rid of the unwanted visitor and eased himself slowly from the low-slung vehicle. By the time he was standing on the gravelled forecourt beads of sweat stood out on his brow.

Matt propelled himself with the assistance of the much-despised crutches to find out what was taking so long. Once he was in a position to get his first proper view of the girl he stopped wondering.

Honey-blonde hair pulled back into a cute ponytail to reveal a simpering smile—that was no way genuine—pinned on a face that was all scrubbed cheeks, innocent big eyes and sexy lips. Then, last but not least—*definitely* not least—there was the body. No anorexic waif, this one; Lara Croft meets the girl next door! In short, the babe of dopes like Joe's collective dreams.

Joe had a vacuous grin on his face. It made Matt feel embarrassed just to look at it; he'd seen sheep that looked more intelligent than his best friend did at this moment! A superior sneer tugged at the corners of his lips. The women in his dreams had more going for them than insipid prettiness.

'Matt,' Joe hailed him. 'Kat here has been stung by a wasp.'

Matt watched sourly as he held the babe's slim arm out for his inspection.

'Bee,' the babe said in a brisk, un-babe-like voice.

Matt found she was looking critically at himself, not Joe. Her eyes were large, clear grey, lushly fringed by dark curling lashes and tilted ever so slightly at the outer corners.

Bimbo, yes…brainless, no… No amount of mascara or cheesy grins could disguise the intelligence lurking in those crystal-clear depths.

'Are you another one from that damned woman's magazine? I've already told your editor where she can stick her story!' He felt a surge of grim satisfaction as he watched her high-voltage smile gutter.

The reference meant nothing to Kat, so she could shake her head in vigorous denial with a clear conscience.

'I've no idea what you're talking about.' His silence oozed disbelief. 'You *are* Matthew Devlin...?' A case of mistaken identity...? The optimist in her soared before his abrasive response brought her crashing down to earth with a thud.

'I know who I am. Who are you?'

Kat blinked several times, and tried not act as if she felt slightly singed by those blazing blue eyes. He was tall without being lanky, broad of shoulder without being bulky, and darkly beautiful in a dangerous Byronic hero sort of way...in short, a knock-out! She felt a spurt of indignation. Why hadn't someone warned her?

In the masculine beauty stakes she'd have rated him, on a scale of one to ten, at a conservative twelve and a half! She couldn't help but reflect that it would have been an aesthetic tragedy if a face like that had been scarred; as it was, the only immediate evidence of his injuries was a thin scar that ran from a point midway along his prominent cheekbone to his temple.

He'd probably laugh when she explained...they'd laugh together. Another look at that lean uncompromising face with its intriguing planes and angles told her that was taking optimism too far! Whatever else this job was going to be, it wasn't going to be a laugh a minute.

To prove that she wasn't intimidated—an uphill battle— she smiled serenely, and the dark fallen angel face didn't budge. There wasn't even the suggestion of a quiver around the beautifully sculpted lips.

Faced with belligerent antagonism on the face of her patient—and Kat was getting the distinct impression this wasn't the sort of man who would respond to gentle understanding—she felt a twinge of nostalgia for the pale, pliable, mummy's boy of her imagination.

There was nothing even faintly pliable about the man

who was looking at her with the sort of affection most folk reserved for something nasty they'd discovered on their shoe! He might be using crutches but nothing about him said vulnerable. Even in less than full working order he exuded an almost tangible aura of restless vitality.

'I'm Kathleen Wray.'

Illness must have taken its toll, but he wasn't making any concessions to it. Probably those lines around his eyes and hard but sexy mouth hadn't been so deeply ingrained before his accident; long-term pain probably had a lot to do with the faint blue smudges under those fairly spectacular eyes too. Those deep-set, heavy-lidded orbs were just as startlingly blue as his mother's, but whereas hers sparkled with humour his held a restless almost explosive quality. In fact there was something combustible about the entire man!

'Is that supposed to mean anything to me?'

'I think maybe the sting's still in,' Joe fretted. 'What are you supposed to use for bee stings—vinegar...?'

The babe firmly repossessed her arm. 'I've got some hydrocortisone cream in my bag.' She dismissed the throb in her arm with a careless shrug.

'And where might your bag be?' Matt asked, looking around for any sign of transport.

'In my room.' Her eyes innocently sought the second-floor window in an effort to locate the charming room she'd been allocated.

The significance of the gesture wasn't lost on Matt. 'Are you trying to tell me you're actually staying here? What the hell's going on?' he barked.

'I assumed you'd be expecting me. I'm your physiotherapist, Mr Devlin.'

'Not the best cover story. I don't have a physiotherapist.'

'You mustn't worry. Your mother...' Matt watched as she gave a self-conscious glance towards Joe. The composed little voice with the husky rasp dropped to a confidential whisper. 'She's paying my salary.'

'*Hah!*' Matt wasn't sure why he should be worried about her salary, but at the mention of his parent things started to make a lot more sense.

His mother was untiring in her determined efforts to fling females she considered suitable mates in his path, in the mistaken belief that a grandchild was the key to healing the rift between father and son.

'My mother. I should have guessed.'

His scrutiny slid over Kat from head to toe in a boldly insolent way that had her chin automatically rising to an aggressive angle.

'Impressive.' His eyes lingered on the contours of her full breasts.

Which was more than could be said for his manners! But Kat could cope with crude sexual innuendo; she had stopped rounding her shoulders in a futile attempt to hide her womanly attributes when she was about fifteen. She squared said shoulders proudly and clung onto her temper with difficulty.

'I'm terminating your contract, Blondie.'

That was the best news she'd heard for some time, and it was on the tip of her tongue to tell him so when she recalled the promise Drusilla had wrung out of her. Concentrating on the state of her debts made it easier to retain her composure.

'My name is Kathleen Wray. You can call me Miss Wray, or, at a push, Kat. I don't answer to *Blondie*. And I'm not leaving until your *mother* tells me my services are no longer required.' Her rigid stance faded as her stormy grey eyes softened. 'Pride is all well and good, Mr Devlin,' she announced in a kindly way. 'But, whether you like it or not—' she cast a swift professional eye over his tall, broad-shouldered figure '—you do need me.'

Matt looked baffled by her response.

'Are you slow or what...?' He didn't need this, not now. He was in pain, hot, tired and had a damned hank of hair in his eyes and no free hand to push it away. As always the mortifying consequences of illness made him mad enough to yell and curse. It took a lot of self-control to restrain his inclination to indulge in both.

'It's probably the pain that's making you so tetchy.' She kept her tone objective, not that it made his reaction any the less hostile. From the way his eyes flashed and his jaw tightened, she assumed he took any reference to his physical weakness as a direct insult; some men were like that.

'I'm not in pain!' Matt bellowed, throwing self-restraint to the winds. The muscles down his left leg chose that precise moment to go into painful spasm. Matt swore under his breath and gritted his teeth against the pain.

'I told you you shouldn't have gone into the office.' There was a concerned note in his friend's voice.

'Save your sanctimonious I-told-you-sos.' Matt closed his eyes and forced himself not to fight the wave of pain. Experience had taught him tensing up only prolonged the spasms.

'You didn't bring him straight here from the hospital...?'

'He wouldn't let me.'

'I really don't see there was much he could do to stop you!' Kat responded crisply.

Her eyes were compassionate as she looked at the tall figure who was obviously suffering considerable pain. When he tried to shrug off the supportive hand she placed beneath his elbow she diplomatically pretended not to notice his efforts to dislodge her light grip.

'You don't know Matt,' Joe returned wryly.

Kat resisted the childish impulse to assure him she didn't want to.

'Let's get him inside, shall we?' Matt heard the bimbo say, just before he had to endure the ultimate indignity of being hustled like a baby through the door between his best friend and Blondie.

Dear God, it had been bad enough when those damned nurses had fussed and fretted; this was more than flesh and blood could be expected to take!

'When did he last take his medication?'

Matt lifted his dark head from the brocade-covered chaise-longue they'd deposited him on. 'What are you asking him for? I'm not dumb!' he snarled.

'We should be so lucky,' his friend breathed quietly.

'What was that, Joe...?' Matt growled.

'When did you last take any pain relief?' You didn't need to be psychic to figure out that wiping the sheen of perspiration from his furrowed brow would not go down well. Fortunately his colour was looking more healthy than it had outside.

Kat's eyes slowly worked their way up the strong column of his throat to his lean, angular face. Though pale after his hospitalisation, Matthew Devlin had the sort of olive skin tones that would darken given the first hint of sunlight.

She had a sudden and deeply distracting image of him stretched out on a beach, his skin gleaming with a healthy glow. She gave her head the tiniest of shakes to dispel the unprofessional hallucination.

She gave a whimsical but worried grin. Just as well he didn't have a personality to match his looks or she might have trouble staying impersonal! If someone had forced her to produce a fantasy lover he would have looked remarkably similar to Matthew Devlin—which just went to show that looks weren't everything!

'I need a drink, not a pill. Pass me a Scotch, Joe.'

Kat wondered if he ever said *please* as she laid a restraining hand on Joe's arm.

'I don't suppose there's any reason you can't have both, but it depends on what sort of painkillers you're taking.'

'I'm not taking pain relief...I don't need crutches of any

sort,' he announced with scornful and not strictly accurate distaste.

Lips compressed into a stubborn white line, he rose to his feet. Deliberately ignoring the crutches and his audience's combined concern, he walked over to the drinks cabinet and poured himself a whisky.

Kat was pretty sure that every step he took was agony, but the only external evidence of this in his drawn face were the beads of sweat that appeared across his upper lip. The man had guts—she had to hand him that. It was just a pity he didn't channel his energies into something more constructive than thumbing his nose at the world in general and her in particular!

He lifted the glass in a mocking salute before downing the amber liquid in one swallow.

'A pill to go to sleep, another to wake...I'm not buying into that merry-go-round. I thought pain was the body's way of telling a person something.'

Matt had been the soul of restraint up until very recently. Even when they hadn't known how bad the spinal damage was, and life in a wheelchair had been a nightmare possibility, he'd managed to retain control of his stiff upper lip.

It had been the killing *slowness* of the whole convalescence thing that had finally made him snap. He was used to setting himself a goal and working towards it; he didn't see why getting back to full fitness should be any different, but the blasted medics were constantly holding him back.

'Going on the evidence so far, I rather doubt you've been listening to your body at all this morning, Mr Devlin.'

She'd seen his type before—though not quite so spectacularly packaged—the sort of man who'd push himself and his body to the limit of endurance and beyond. That sort of willpower was all very laudable, and probably made the person successful at anything he set his mind to—but it also made him a terrible patient!

'My mother may think I need the attentions of some sultry little nursey...'

To Kat's intense discomfort he did that undressing thing with his eyes again. She didn't doubt for a second it was meant to unsettle her, but she'd not give him the satisfaction of showing how well the crude tactics worked.

'...but I can assure you I don't. So ignoring the fact I've fired you isn't going to change my mind.'

It wasn't a comfortable experience being pinned down by those arrogant eyes but Kat knew it would be fatal to back down at this point. However, facing down this man was proving to be one of the hardest things she'd ever done. It made her shudder to think how difficult it would be to thwart him when he was fully fit. She didn't think she'd ever come across anyone who had such an ingrained aura of command.

'I'm a physio, not a nurse.'

'If you say so...'

Did the man think she was pretending, for God's sake? Kat repressed the strong inclination to dig out her certificates and wave them under his infuriating nose.

'Ignoring the fact you've got pain isn't going to make it go away,' she responded serenely.

Did she think he didn't know that? Matt ground his teeth.

'And being rude and unreasonable isn't going to make me go away, either. I've worked with some very difficult children...'

A choking noise emerged from Joe's throat. Matt was too stunned to notice his friend's heaving shoulders.

'Are you suggesting I'm acting like a *child*?' he grated incredulously.

'You're only a child to your mother, Mr Devlin,' she explained kindly. 'To me you're simply a client.'

The little witch was patronising him! The fact she looked like a fantasy figure made the fact she acted like a damned nanny all the more unpalatable. What sort of underwear did a nanny-pin-up hybrid wear—naughty black lace or prissy white cotton? His mental preoccupation with her damned underwear represented yet another example of his diminished mental control to Matt.

'Client?' he snarled. 'A fancy name for a patient! Bloody doctors!' he yelled, his frustration showing. 'What do they know…?'

Hell! Why not go the whole way and stamp your feet, Matt? Small wonder her smile had a definite smug tinge to it. What, he wondered, had happened to the man of few words—none of them sulky—who could alter the course of a high-powered meeting with an effortlessly enigmatic look? It was humiliating to be forced to recognise he'd substituted infantile for enigmatic!

'About flying a helicopter, probably nothing,' she soothed. Matt was beginning to be able to predict the precise moment that dimple would peep out. 'About relieving pain, hopefully quite a lot. It might seem very macho to suffer in silence, but there's nothing particularly clever about suffering when there's no need. There's no disgrace in admitting you need help.' With a small frown, her critical eyes ran over his stubbornly erect figure. If he'd ever had any excess flesh on his greyhound lean frame, it had been burned off long ago. 'Actually, I'm surprised they discharged you so soon.'

'So soon?' he blasted. The memory of weeks and months of immobility was still in sharp focus in his mind as glared with intense dislike at the interfering female his mother had seen fit to inflict upon him.

'They didn't discharge him,' Joe volunteered. 'Though I suspect they might be breathing a large collective sigh of relief about now. You'll probably find this hard to believe, but he was the perfect patient up until about three weeks ago… Uncomplaining, charming…'

'Displaying the desired degree of dog-like obedience…' Matt cut in savagely.

'You're right, I do find it hard to believe.'

Matt glanced at her sharply. So Miss Sugar and Spice had claws, he mused thoughtfully. The discovery made her slightly less objectionable...*very* slightly.

'Then almost overnight it was bye-bye Mr Nice Guy! I suppose everyone has their breaking point, even Matt Devlin.'

'I think you're rather overplaying the irony,' Matt growled darkly.

'You always have had a problem with delegating, haven't you, Matt?' Joe observed, with an innocent smile. 'I think he'd have secretly preferred it if his empire had crumbled without him at the helm.'

Matt glared at his oldest friend with intense dislike.

Kat found the talk of empires—a private joke, maybe—a bit confusing, but what she did understand from this interchange brought a deep furrow to her wide smooth brow.

'So he discharged himself against medical advice...?' Drusilla had said nothing about that!

'*What if I did?*' Matt asked belligerently. 'And, if it's not too much bother, do you mind not talking about me in the third person? I've had it up to here—' he jabbed his hand up against his forehead, which did nothing to improve his headache, and almost made him lose his balance '—with medical busybodies! There's nothing more anyone else, no matter how many medical degrees they've got, can do for me now. Anything that happens from this point onwards is up to me.'

Kat's worried frown grew more pronounced. If he wasn't prepared to accept limitations he could put back his recovery months.

'I'll have to talk to your doctor,' she announced decisively. 'What's his name?'

'Hasn't it sunk in yet, baby-face? I fired you. Come to that, I never even employed you!'

'I'm not working for you; I'm working for Drusilla.'

'Drusilla,' Matt drawled with a cynical smile. 'How cosy.'

'Metcalf. His doctor's called Metcalf.'

Joe decided the angel's smile was well worth the murderous glare he received from Matt.

'And the clinic is...?'

'There's a name for friends like you,' Matt announced grimly when the so-called physio had whisked busily away to have a heart-to-heart with his doctor.

Joe smiled unrepentantly back. 'Sorry old son. Why don't you sit down?' he suggested. '*I* already know you're made of steel,' he added slyly as Matt limped over to an armchair. 'It strikes me, Matt, you're being awkward for the sake of it. You said yourself what a pain it was going to be traipsing off to the local hospital for physio every other day.'

'I'm quite capable of employing my own physio. And if the babe doesn't go, I will! I don't have to stay here,' he railed. 'If my place has got too many steps I'll buy another one. I've no intention of going along with one of my mother's little schemes.'

Joe grinned. 'She just wants to see you with a good woman.'

Matt's expression grew even more cynical. 'Of her choosing.'

'Well, maybe she's got a point. Delegating the task might not be such a bad idea...not with your track record. I mean, what man in his right mind would get engaged to Angela!'

'I wasn't engaged to Angela, except in her fevered imagination.'

'You know that, I know that, but thousands of readers of the popular press think you're an object of pity.'

'Thanks for that, Joe. I feel better already,' Matt came back, dry as dust.

'You've had your chance to set the record straight,' Joe reminded him, tongue firmly in his cheek.

A scornful sound escaped Matt's throat. 'I'd prefer to slit my throat than become a human interest story in a women's magazine.' There was genuine horror in his eyes.

'How can you be so sure she isn't genuine…?'

Matt gave a derisive snort. 'You have a charmingly naïve view of women, Joe. I think I almost envy you…'

'I'm not bitter and twisted, and proud of it,' Joe added with a touch of lazy defiance.

'You're just a sucker for a pretty face…'

'*Pretty* doesn't really do her justice.'

'I find it hard to see past the simpering smile.'

Kat's bosom swelled with indignation—she'd never simpered in her life! Her fingers tightened around the door-handle.

'Matt!' Joe ejaculated, shocked by the irreverence.

Matt remained unrepentant. 'My mother is totally unscrupulous when it comes to getting what she wants, and at the moment she wants a grandchild. She's always thought no man can resist a cleavage.' His expression was grim as he reflected on the callous machinations of his manipulative parent.

'To tell you the truth, Matt, as far as cleavages go I've always thought much the same myself.' Joe admitted.

Despite the pain he was enduring, Matt's lips twitched. 'Under that choir-boy façade, Joe Casey, there lurks the soul of a debauched swine.'

'Chance would be a fine thing. You can't tell me you don't find her at all attractive?' Joe regarded his friend with open scepticism.

On the point of walking in, Kat paused. She found her own hesitation predictable and pathetic, but what girl, she reasoned, could resist hearing whether a man—even if she didn't like him—found her fanciable…?

'She's got all the right equipment, but it's the cabbage scenario.'

'Cabbage?' Joe's tone echoed the sort of bewilderment Kat was feeling.

'During my formative years everyone—nannies, parents, schoolteachers—they were all constantly telling me how good it was for me. Naturally I developed a loathing for the stuff which lasts to this day.'

'So you want a woman who is bad for you?'

'You're missing the point, Joe. I don't want one someone thinks I *should* want.'

That was what you get for eavesdropping! Kat had never been likened to cabbage before—she'd have remembered.

She wouldn't have been human if she hadn't allowed her mind to dwell on the pleasant picture of Matt Devlin a helpless victim of her irresistible charms. It would have been petty to dwell for too long on the image of his despair when she rejected him.

His antagonism made perfect sense now. No wonder he was acting like a real pain in the posterior if he thought his mother had sent her here to land a husband! This was an embarrassing mistake she could easily correct.

Her upbeat expression as she walked into the room didn't even hint that she cared about the cabbage thing.

'You've got it all wrong. I don't want to marry you... For heaven's sake, I don't even like you!'

CHAPTER TWO

THERE was a startled pause during which Kat prayed for the ground to open up and swallow her. It didn't, and she was left wondering why she'd imagined for a second that matters would be improved by telling a man she couldn't stand the sight of him!

'That must be a weight off your mind, Matt.' Joe's voice quivered ever so slightly.

Straight from the heart! The muscles of Matt's throat worked overtime as he fought back unexpected laughter... Watching her face fall as she realised what she'd just said struck him as one of the funniest things he'd seen in ages... But then, if his nearest and dearest were to be believed, he had a particularly warped sense of humour.

'I have to tell you there are some serious flaws in your seduction technique, Miss Wray.' The gibe was delivered in a manner that suggested he was generously offering her advice.

He didn't normally get a kick out of seeing people grovel, but there were exceptions...! No man, no matter how secure he was, liked being told a beautiful woman didn't fancy him. He speculated—in a lazy, objective kind of way—how hard it would be to make her change her mind. Rejection didn't occur to Matt.

Kat's cheeks grew hotter as she squirmed under his malicious scrutiny... So she'd put both feet in it. It wasn't very charitable of him to labour the fact...and enjoy it so much!

'If you automatically assume every woman you meet is out to seduce you, perhaps you need the services of a good

psychologist, not a physio!' Go on, Kat, you tell him; it's
not as if you *need* the job, is it?

Matt met her defiant glare with a thoughtful expression.
So, no grovelling.

She braced herself, pretty sure he was going to say something blighting, and pretty sure she deserved it, but when
those heavy lids lifted he just stared... Kat had never personally encountered a stare quite like this. She found she
could readily visualise innocent men confessing to heinous
crimes if forced to endure that expressionless intensity for
too long! She was glad that the only thing she was guilty
of was clumsiness!

'It's not personal or anything.'

His sardonic stare underlined the stupidity of her stilted
announcement.

'I mean, I'm sure you're a very nice person...*underneath*...' Underneath being a dyed-in-the-wool misogynist,
that was.

Was this meant to soothe his bruised ego...? Nobody as
far as Matt could recall had ever called him 'nice' before
as if they meant it, let alone as if they didn't mean it!

The dangerous glitter in his eyes made Kat feel even
more flustered. She decided it might be a good time to
change tack.

'I suppose you think it's odd that Drusilla didn't tell you
about me... Actually,' she conceded truthfully, 'I do too.'

'I'm sure she had her reasons.'

Kat tried to ignore the nasty *knowing* note in his voice
and racked her brains for a reasonable explanation to account for Drusilla Devlin's strange behaviour in dropping
her in it like this.

'She was probably worried you wouldn't want me,' she
mused half to herself.

That had a nice self-effacing note to it. A cynical smile
twisted his lips as Matt's eyes slowly travelled the length

of her curvaceous figure; this wasn't a woman who lay awake at nights worrying about rejection.

Kat continued her meandering explanation, oblivious to his cynical observations.

'I really needed the job you see.' It was probably way too late to remember that.

Now there was a statement that just begged a question, and if he asked it he'd have laid money on her being able to produce a first-class sob story... Ironically, he was half inclined to believe it might even be true! If this was acting, it was Oscar-class stuff.

'Simple philanthropy rarely covers my mother's behaviour...'

'It's true,' Kat fired back, angry on Drusilla's behalf. 'Your mother was being *kind* to me, offering me the job...not that I'm not very well qualified.' She frowned fiercely and divided her glare that said she was willing to defend her credentials between both men. 'You see, she went to school with my mum and she knew I was in a bit of a fix...moneywise...' An uncomfortable flush mounted her smooth cheeks as she hastily skipped over this subject.

'I can't help but feel it might have been simpler all round if she'd just given you the money, not foisted you on me.'

Kat's eyes widened in indignation. 'I don't take charity!'

'A girl with principles,' he drawled.

'You find that funny?' she snapped from between clenched teeth.

'I find it commendable,' he replied with such patent insincerity that Kat felt like hitting him over the head with one of his crutches. She didn't normally have such violent inclinations, but he was an *extremely* trying man.

'I'm more than capable of working for my money...'

'And is this...project paying very well?'

This was one nasty insinuation too many, as far as Kat was concerned. 'Let's just say that I'd need to be getting an awful lot more if the job description included trying to get romantic with you! I don't mean to be rude—'

'You do surprise me—'

'—but you did ask,' she finished defiantly. 'And I don't know why you're acting so offended. Nobody's suggested *you're* stupid and avaricious enough to agree to marry someone if you were paid enough!'

'I don't think my mother paid you.'

He didn't add that the prospect of being his wife would be financial inducement enough for a lot of women... Maybe not this woman...? Definitely not this woman! It had been some time since he'd met a starry-eyed idealist, which no doubt accounted for the fact it had taken him so long to recognise this one. In his opinion, idealism was a dangerously unpredictable trait.

Her brows shot up in elaborate surprise. 'You think I'd do it for free?' she flung back childishly.

For the first time she glimpsed a flicker of genuine humour in his electric blue eyes.

'I think she was relying on propinquity and my natural charm to do the job,' he responded drily. He smiled and provided her with a brief but dazzling flash of that charm. 'You look dubious...but, you see, mothers,' he explained gravely, 'are notoriously blind when it comes to their offspring.'

'I didn't mean to be—'

Matt waved aside her protest with a faint movement of his long tapering fingers. 'Personal...I know. For someone who is keen on professional detachment, you cram in more insults per minute than anyone else I've ever met.'

'But...'

'Calm down, that's not bad.'

'It isn't?'

'I can't abide boot-lickers,' he announced blandly. 'Let's say for one minute that you can swear hand on heart—' his focus shifted to the region where that organ was housed, and lingered there '—that you're only here to continue the torture inflicted on me by members of your profession in the clinic.'

Kat let out a silent sigh of relief as his eyes finally lifted. She just hoped and prayed her top was thick enough to hide the tingling activity of her nipples.

'That doesn't alter the fact that if I decide I need a resident nurse or physio I'd prefer one of my own choosing...'

Kat was still too preoccupied by the inexplicable behaviour of her body to summon up the necessary energy to fight him on this; besides, as much as she needed this job, she wasn't about to beg.

'It won't take me long to pack.' She made a conscious effort to belatedly put a bit of dignity back into the proceedings. Actually, some things were worse than being in debt—things like being eaten up with lust for a man you didn't even like!

'I thought you needed the job...?'

Anyone would think he gave a damn! Kat fixed him with an angry incredulous stare. He definitely was the most perverse man she'd ever encountered.

'She does, she does...'

Kat had almost forgotten the other man's presence.

'Your concern for my well-being is touching, Joe. I'm well aware that it wouldn't suit your plans if I went for a male physio built like a barn...' Matt taunted his lust-sick friend with idle affection.

Joe blushed and glanced uncomfortably in Kat's direction. 'If you weren't ill...'

'Don't sulk in front of the lady, Joseph...'

'I wasn't sulking!'

Kat, happy to be distracted from the wantonly indiscriminate behaviour of her own body, gave a weak indulgent smile as she watched the two men good-naturedly bicker; the rapport between them obviously went deep.

An extraordinary notion occurred to her, and her jaw

dropped as her eyes darted rapidly from one man to the other and back again. It couldn't be, *could it*? As unlikely as the explanation seemed, it would explain why his mother felt Matt wasn't going to get a wife without a lot of encouragement.

'Heavens, I didn't realise!' she blurted out, without thinking. Her mind was racing. Why hadn't that possibility occurred to her before? After all, one of the most masculine, *straight*-looking men she knew was gay.

'Realise what?' Matt asked

'It's all right,' she explained soothingly. 'One of my best friends is gay, and his parents found it hard to accept at first too, but they came round eventually and...'

'Gay!' Joe, his eyes round, looked at his hand, innocently resting on Matt's shoulder, and with a horrified snort jerked it away.

Kat smiled in what she hoped was an open-minded non-judgmental sort of way as she tried to analyse her somewhat ambivalent response to this discovery. There didn't seem any harm now to acknowledge that the prospect of treating a man who she found so physically attractive—in a butterflies-in-the-belly...*tingly* sort of way—had been bothering her. She ought to be feeling much happier...much less cheated... *Cheated?* Where had that come from?

She kept her attention carefully trained on Joe. 'You don't owe me any explanations,' she told him warmly.

Joe looked with smouldering resentment at his friend who, after a startled pause, had begun laughing.

'This is your fault,' he accused wildly. 'I told you you should have got a haircut.'

'I had no idea that sexual orientation had any direct connection with hair length.'

'Stop mucking around, will you?' Joe yelled. *'Tell her...we're not!'*

'It's no good, Joe, she's guessed!' Matt intoned dramatically.

'Cut it out, Matt!' Joe begged, looking slightly sick. He felt unable to take this slur on his masculinity as lightly as his friend seemed to.

It was slowly dawning on Kat that yet again she'd jumped to the wrong conclusion.

'Oh, God!' she groaned. 'I've got it wrong, haven't I?'

'Sorry, Miss Wray, but we're both strictly hetero…' If she got any redder there was a good chance she'd spontaneously combust, he thought, watching her discomfort with a degree of spiteful pleasure.

'This could be a double bluff to get me where you want me…' Matt mused thoughtfully.

Which presumably was flat on his back and helpless! The mental image that accompanied this maverick thought of her astride his prone body had enough detail to deepen the colour in her already pink cheeks significantly. She didn't normally fantasise about having a man at her mercy!

'But I'm inclined to give you the benefit of the doubt.'

Kat's mouth fell ajar with shock and dismay. *'You are?'*

'Unless, of course, you want to reveal that you actually find me and this broken body irresistible…?' It bothered him like hell to detect the faint note of self-pity in his voice. As far as he was concerned, self-pity had no constructive value and therefore no place in his life. Self-pity was for losers.

'Heavens!' Kat exclaimed, so thoroughly thrown off balance by this remarkable change in his attitude that she forgot about professional reticence.

'Dr Metcalf forgot to mention your mood swings.'

It was what he hadn't forgotten to tell her that interested Matt, whose eyes narrowed to suspicious slits.

'Sounds like good old Andrew was very obliging…'

With an exasperated sigh, Kat planted her hands on her softly rounded hips. A little toss of her head made the honey-gold ponytail dance in a way that charmed at least one of the men watching her performance.

'Don't start with that again, or I'm out of here...' God, when will I learn to control my tongue? If he called her bluff, the schedule she'd worked out to repay the last of the debts would have to go out of the window. She crossed her fingers firmly.

'Is that a threat or a promise?'

Kat heaved a sigh of relief. 'Your mother had warned him that I'd probably be ringing...'

'That's Mum, all right. She thinks of everything.'

Kat loftily ignored this acid interjection. 'As I was saying,' she continued frostily, 'Dr Metcalf merely supplied me with *medical* details.' She didn't mention that during the course of their telephone conversation the doctor's grudging admiration for his patient had come across clearly.

'It's always handy to know that someone is likely to throw a wobbler if you mention *wheelchair,*' she added slyly.

She let this sink in for a moment and watched from under the sweep of her lashes for Matt's reaction. A slow grin slowly spread over his face; it filled his eyes with an unexpected and dangerously attractive warmth.

'Do you *really* think you're such a great catch?' she grouched.

So it wasn't tactful, but a girl had her breaking point! And it was something that Kat felt needed saying; this man had an entirely too great an opinion of himself! So what if he had a smile that could melt a girl's bones?

Matt wasn't a vain man, but he did take some things for granted and one of them was, to put it crudely—as Joe had, on more than one occasion—his *pulling power*! Without realising it, over the years he had come to expect a certain degree of appreciation from females.

It wasn't as if he had any illusions about what attracted many women, and in Matt's view it wasn't the fascination

of his blue eyes! He had money and power, and a particular
sort of woman liked men who could provide them with
those things. How else did you explain hordes of drop-dead
gorgeous lovelies on the arms of men old enough to be
their grandfathers?

Despite normally evincing a healthy cynicism for that
sort of adulation, now, reading the scorn in Kat's wide eyes,
he decided that uncritical worship might not be so bad after
all! Just how hard, he speculated, his lips settling into a
brooding line of dissatisfaction, would it be to replace that
superior disdain with indiscriminate drooling desire...?
Now *that* might be the sort of therapy he needed!

'You were going, I think, Joseph,' Matt said without taking his eyes off Kat.

'I was...?' It occurred to Joe that, as far as the woman
of his dreams was concerned, he had never really been there
at all—he tried to take the fact he wasn't making any con-
tribution towards the electric atmosphere in the room phil-
osophically.

'Don't worry, I think I'll be quite safe in Miss Wray's
capable hands.'

Matt couldn't ignore the stimulating effect this the image
had on his jaded imagination... It was the undies question
rearing its ugly head again. Were lingerie fetishes a normal
result of several months of enforced celibacy...? There
could be a paper in this for good old Dr Metcalf...

Kat could hardly believe the startling alteration in his
manner. He sounded suspiciously like a normal, rational
human being; there was even a hint of beguiling warmth
in his voice!

'You don't mind me being here?' Kat discovered she felt
rather ambivalent about this breakthrough. She did have the
offer of several temporary beds... Would you really prefer
to be a burden on your friends? she asked herself sternly.

'I want to throw those—' his electric blue gaze lit momentarily on the discarded crutches '—out for good. If you

can speed up the process I'd be a fool to object, wouldn't I.'

It *sounded* reasonable...

'Yes, you would.' It seemed that he was no longer fearful that she would seduce him... How did you go about seducing someone...? With her rudimentary grasp of the subject, she'd probably produce a seduction routine that would have him laughing some more. She still felt like wincing when she thought about the sound of his deep, uninhibited amusement at her expense.

'Then that's settled.'

'Your mother said that you—'

Matt didn't much want to know what his mother said. 'I thought you two were on first-name terms...?' Matt interrupted her flow.

'Is that a problem, Mr Devlin?'

'Nobody calls me Mr Devlin.'

Kat's mobile features screwed up in an uneasy frown. 'I'm not sure I'm comfortable using your first name...' She wasn't sure why she felt so strongly about this... It wasn't as if she was renowned for her formality.

'I'm sure we all want you to be comfortable...' he responded smoothly.

Then why, she wondered, does everything you do appear to be specifically designed to make me feel uneasy...? 'No, I'm sure it will be fine...Matthew...'

'Matt. And you're...?'

'Kat.'

'Which is short for what...? Katherine...?'

'Kathleen,' she supplied, feeling a strange reluctance to divulge any personal information, no matter how innocuous, to this man.

'Kathleen... Irish...?'

When he wasn't barking orders or sounding paranoid, Matthew Devlin had a sinfully attractive voice, the sort of voice that had a colour and texture—in this case, midnight-blue and velvet—when you closed your eyes to appreciate the husky resonance. Kat didn't close her eyes, but it was a close call!

'On my mother's side,' she confirmed.

'Me, too.'

'I know. They went to school together, but they hadn't seen each other for years and years,' she added swiftly, in case it got him started on the conspiracy theory again. 'Not until…recently.'

Matt didn't need to be hit on the head with evasion to recognise it. He'd always been good at picking up on things people didn't say; it was a trait that had done him no harm in his business dealings. He felt his curiosity stir as he wondered about what Kat was leaving unsaid.

Kat was sorry to see Joe go. She'd felt he might be a useful ally in hostile territory. Kat was realistic; she had her foot in the door, but she was pretty sure that this was only the first hurdle—she soon discovered her instincts were right.

'I'll use the room I always do, thank you, Elizabeth. If you could have my bags moved upstairs at some point I'd be grateful.' Despite the pleasant smile he had for the housekeeper, there was no doubt Matt hadn't liked discovering he'd been put in the ground-floor guest suite.

The housekeeper, whom Kat had had down as the unemotional type, had all but wept with joy at seeing Matt. There was no accounting for taste! She now cast a look of urgent appeal in Kat's direction as she left the room.

The door closed and Kat could no longer keep a hold on her tongue. She was too exasperated by this point to wrap up her criticism in sugar-coated terms. So far, during their cosy *getting to know one another* chat, he had vetoed every tentative suggestion she'd made, for no reason as far as she could see other than pig-headed awkwardness, plain and simple.

'I suppose that's one way to prove you're in control. Lay

down the law, watch them jump and don't worry,' she soothed nastily. 'Even if they think what you're saying is stupid they're not likely to say so!'

Kat had never met a more obstinate individual! For the life of her she couldn't understand why the staff here seemed so delighted to have him staying—it was bizarre. The housekeeper in particular seemed a very sensible woman, which made her reaction to Matt all the more incomprehensible.

Perhaps the man had hidden depths…? No, Kat decided, with an angry sniff, if he did have depths they were probably murky. Either it was case of mass hypnotism or the whole place must be particularly susceptible to blue eyes; there was no other explanation.

The thought drew her own angry eyes back to his. There was no escaping the fact that his eyes were *very* blue. Kat herself had found her own gaze repeatedly drawn towards his thickly lashed deep-set eyes as their conversation had become increasingly one-sided. Right now, the main expression she could see in those azure depths was shock… Perhaps he didn't expect the paid help to answer back?

Matt settled back in his seat and reached for a slice of carrot cake, looked at it with a look as jaded as his palate, and then put it back on the plate untouched.

'I take it I shouldn't expect you to feel equally stifled when it comes to the subject of my stupidity.'

'Are you going to eat that?'

'Why, do you want it?' He held out the plate towards her. So far she'd gone through two slices and several of the wafer-thin smoked salmon sandwiches.

'Very funny.' Her lips twisted with impatience. 'You never think about other people, do you?'

'Not feeling hungry puts me in the selfish and heartless category…?' Why was he surprised? She seemed able to imbue his most innocent action with sinister intent. 'Your logic is interesting—bizarre, but interesting.' Interlacing his fingers, he rested his square chin thoughtfully on them. 'I feel sure you're about to fill in the gaps for me.'

'The afternoon tea.' She waved her hand over the rather grand spread. 'I bet everything here is your favourite,' she accused.

Kat watched as his blue eyes swept over the food on the delicate china plates. Now that she'd pointed it out, he recognised favoured titbits from his schooldays. His shoulders lifted in a negligent concessionary shrug.

'Hah! I'm right!' she crowed.

'If you've got a point to make, I think now is the time to make it.'

'You don't see, do you?' She shook her head disapprovingly. 'A lot of people went to a great deal of trouble to do something nice for you, because for some reason they seem to care about you. How do you think they're going to feel if this lot goes back the kitchen untouched...?'

The troubled frown that flickered across his face was barely discernible before his expression grew impatient. 'I haven't liked sweet things since I was twelve years old.'

Her arms folded across her chest and she wondered whether he had a better nature to appeal to. 'You don't like...and I suppose that makes it all right to ride roughshod over people's feelings?'

His narrowed blue eyes drilled into her. 'We're not talking cakes here, are we?'

'Your mother has gone to a lot of trouble specially preparing those rooms for you.'

This was obviously the point where he was meant to be overcome by remorse and self-loathing.

'My mother isn't going to lose any sleep over where I choose to sleep,' he drawled languidly.

'Well, if you're not bothered about hurting Drusilla's feelings...'

'You have a nasty habit of putting words into a man's mouth...' His eyes dwelt for a long distracted moment on the lush curves of her kissable lips... Other things might taste more palatable on his tongue than her acid recriminations.

'Consider the practicalities. Just how exactly do you expect to get upstairs to your usual bedroom?' she asked him.

'Crawl...?' Tact and compassion had their place, but not when dealing with Matt Devlin. Empathy wasn't going to get her anywhere with this man, but brutal practicality might.

She wanted to play hard ball...fine. Matt suspected he'd had more practice at the pastime than Blondie here.

'I can't carry you. I suppose you could employ some muscular young man...'

'I thought we'd already established I'm not into muscular young men...' he drawled.

Kat ignored this interruption designed to distract her, even though the reminder made her flush. 'But I expect your mother thought you'd prefer to be more independent.'

'You think I'm ungrateful...?' With a twisted smile he watched her struggle with the temptation to rip his character to shreds some more.

'I've seen the suite, and it's conveniently close to the pool and gym... Nothing could be more suitable.'

Or decadent, at least as far as the leisure facilities were concerned. The Roman-styled pool-house complete with waterfall which had been converted from a stable block had taken Kat's breath away and made her want to tear off her clothes and immerse herself in that warm inviting water... Considering what had happened, it seemed ironic that back then she'd been concerned about first impressions—being caught skinny-dipping hadn't seemed to capture the right note!

Kat was too startled to even squeak in protest when his hand shot out and he jerked her towards the chair he sat in. Off balance, she came down heavily on one knee; she only prevented herself from falling any further by bracing a hand against the arm of his chair.

'Is there some constructive reason you keep reminding I'm an invalid?'

She took a couple of steadying breaths and inhaled undiluted Matt scent—it was an earthy, all-male fragrance. A wave fresh of dizziness struck Kat; this man must have cornered the market in pheromones.

Her eyes slid to the fingers encircling her wrist. They were long and lean like the rest of him; their iron strength didn't feel at all sickly to her... She, on the other hand, didn't feel so great at all. Thready, over-fast pulse, sweaty palms—both of which he'd probably noticed—a churning sick feeling in the pit of her stomach. A wave of intense heat raised her body heat several uncomfortable degrees.

'You're not an invalid, but for the moment whether you like it or not you do have limitations...' Relief washed over her. Against all the odds she'd hit just the right note of objectivity and caring.

The slight imperious tilt of his dark head was a concessionary gesture—at least, for the sake of harmony, that was the way she decided to construe it.

Their eyes clashed and the harmony theory fell apart. Kat's ferociously pumping heart sent a surge of adrenaline around her body so fast she felt light-headed.

'So, incidentally, do I.' This time her voice had a faint faraway quality. The focus of her troubled gaze shifted significantly to the fingers still encircling her wrist.

Her hot vision blurred so that for a moment she couldn't quite make out the defining line between his flesh and her own paler skin; the weak fluttery sensations low in her belly got stronger and more disturbing. It was all she could do to stop herself tearing her hand away.

'And one of them is look, but don't touch...?' His extended thumb moved thoughtfully over the blue-veined inner aspect of her wrist. It must be the challenge—he'd never been able to resist one of those—that conjured up the fantasy image of Kat begging him to touch her.

The sweeping motion must have crossed over a sensitive nerve-ending because the sharp electrical thrill Kat felt shot along her arm in both directions.

His hand fell away and her delicately curved eyebrows drew into a perplexed line as a wave of relief way out of proportion with the event washed over her. She felt pretty foolish on her knees, but, given the fact she wasn't sure if she had total control over her limbs, she didn't have much choice but to stay put.

'I can't stop people looking,' she admitted huskily.

'So you can lay those pretty hands on me as much as you like.' One dark brow lifted before he impatiently flicked a heavy section of dark collar-length hair from his eyes. 'But if I reciprocate you'll...?'

What would she do...? It was a purely academic speculation. Up until this moment he hadn't even thought about sex... He'd forgotten what a distraction it could be, *thinking*... He was thinking a lot all of a sudden. He blamed it on that responsive quiver he'd felt run through her body when he'd touched her. So the lovely Kathleen wasn't being quite honest when she'd said she didn't fancy him... *Interesting*.

'I'll think you've fallen for my fatal charm,' she suggested acidly. 'We can all live in hope.'

Her snappy sarcasm lifted his brooding frown and brought a genuine grin to his face.

Despite her best efforts to remain dispassionate, Kat was charmed.

'I always think that *hope* has an unpleasantly passive sound to it...'

Kat didn't need telling that she was in the presence of a man who didn't lie around hoping for things to happen; she was quite sure that he went out and made them happen.

Everything about him said he needed to be in control of his own fate.

'It's a harmless way to while away a wet afternoon though.'

Even though Matt deeply despised the soft-focus image that lodged in his brain of her staring through some rain-drenched window he had to admit it was an absurdly attractive one.

'And what do you hope for during those wet afternoons, Kathleen?'

He had the sort of voice that could effortlessly make a girl believe he could fulfil all her hopes. Her eyes widened with alarm as the stray thought just popped into her head from God knew where!

'The usual things,' she responded, gruffly evasive.

'Like a husband, children, nice house in the suburbs…?' he speculated. 'The traditional female things.'

His patronising attitude really got under her skin. 'Those being things that no man worthy of his testosterone would desire…?'

'How many teenage boys would list becoming a father as one of their ambitions…?' One dark brow quirked scornfully when she didn't respond. His broad shoulders lifted expressively. 'I rest my case.'

'It's just as well one gender feels the urge to procreate or the human race wouldn't last long.'

'Men feel urges, all right, but it's impregnation and not procreation that drives them,' he explained crudely.

Kat felt herself blush like an adolescent; the fact her blushes seemed to amuse him only intensified her discomfort. She couldn't figure out how what had started out as a perfectly innocent conversation had degenerated into something so uncomfortable.

'Perhaps I have a higher regard for your own sex than you do.'

'Then more fool you, Kat. Fidelity is an alien concept to the vast majority of men.'

'Perhaps, Mr Devlin, you judge all men by your own failings...'

'I'm an arrogant male, Kat. What makes you imagine I think I've got any failings?' he drawled. His deep laughter rang out once more before his brows drew into a disapproving line. 'And I thought we'd dispensed with the *Mr Devlin.*'

Kat's tongue ran nervously over the outline of her dry lips.

'Do I make you nervous, Kathleen?'

Wasn't that the idea?

It was the one question she would have liked to avoid, and he'd made her face it. Resentment reflected in her eyes, she met his deceptively innocent blue gaze warily... He made her incredibly jumpy and had done from the first moment.

'It's hardly surprising that I don't feel comfortable,' she responded carefully. 'You've made it quite clear I'm here under sufferance.'

Casually he flicked her softly rounded chin. 'When you know me better...'

'I can hardly wait!' she mumbled.

Her face averted, Kat brushed some invisible specks off the dark grey trousers she wore beneath a white tee-shirt. She rose smoothly to her feet. It ought to give at least the illusion of superiority to look down at him... It didn't. The slow charismatic grin that split his lean face held her dismayed gaze as surely as Superglue.

'You'll know I'm not big on forbearance. You're not here because I feel charitable. It'll be interesting to find out if you're half as good as you say you are...' He watched the colour mount in her cheeks. 'Professionally speaking, of course,' he added smoothly.

She couldn't wait to prove her worth to this sarcastic

swine... Of course, if she could have done it from the com-
parative safety of the neighbouring county, she'd have been
even more eager! Inexplicably, she couldn't concentrate all
that well in the same room as him... Inexplicable, my foot!
a small derisive voice in her head scoffed. You can't keep
your eyes off him and you're worried to death you won't
be able to hide it when things get tactile.

'When did you have in mind?' she asked, her voice brisk
to the point of brusqueness. 'I'll need to assess your capabilities, to begin with,' she explained stolidly, 'and work
out a schedule that suits us....'

Matt rose with creditable style to his feet, unassisted.
'There's plenty of time for that later...' He turned his wrist
and glanced at the metal-banded wristwatch. His eyes
moved to the antique gilded ormolu clock set on the man-
telshelf. 'Still slow,' he confirmed, comparing the two
times. 'I knocked it off with a football when I was a kid;
it's never kept time since.'

In her mind's eye Kat softened the hard angles of his
face and came up with a soft childish version. Had he been
a serious little boy, or a bit wild...?

'I'm afraid I'm expecting some visitors...business. Later,
I'm all yours.' There was nothing childlike or innocent
about the gleam in his eyes.

'There are a lot of things we need to discuss,' she
choked, pulling her wayward imagination in line—it wasn't
easy.

'Discuss away...I can give you three minutes.'

'How kind,' she bit back acidly. 'I'd better talk fast then,
hadn't I? For starters, what hours do you expect me to
work? When is my free time...?'

'You've not started yet and you're already asking for a
day off...!' He shook his head in mock reproof. 'What happened to stamina? What happened to dedication?'

'What happened to reasonable working conditions?' she
came back smartly. 'I already feel as if I've been on duty

for a twenty-four-hour stretch…' Just talking to this man was amongst the most exhausting things she'd ever done. *'I wonder why?'* No wonder Drusilla had laughed when she'd said she'd earn her money!

'Fine; let's get down to basics. I'm flexible. I don't like to tie myself down to specific times; I like people around me to be flexible too.'

'Which means what, exactly?'

'Which means I need you to be on twenty-four-hour call.'

Have no time to call her own? Be at his beck and call night and day with no time off for good behaviour…? That was *so* not on!

'I think you'll find they abolished slavery some time ago.'

'I'll pay you well…if you're good enough.'

'Your mother is paying me,' she reminded him.

'I'll treble whatever she's giving you.'

'That's absurd!' she gasped.

'But tempting?'

Kat's anger intensified. He sounded as if he thought everyone had a price. 'It's not a matter of money.'

'I thought that you were broke?' he reminded her languidly. 'To lie well, you need a good memory.'

'I wasn't lying!' she flared. 'I am broke.'

'Then I'm the answer to your prayers.'

'Your touching modesty must make you friends wherever you go,' she gasped, unable to totally repress the quiver of amusement in her voice… The man had arrogance off the scale. 'You may not need to sleep…'

'*Need* doesn't enter into it. I *can't* sleep, full stop.'

He looked just as surprised that he'd told her this as she had been to hear him admit it. Insomnia implied a weakness and, as far as she could tell, Matt didn't admit to those.

'What did the doctor say…?' she began.

'I thought I'd made my opinion of drugs clear

to you...' He looked as though he wouldn't need much encouragement to tell her again.

'You have. There are other ways to treat insomnia.'

'*I know*.... Then perhaps we should compare notes.' She didn't need the addition of his suggestive, husky laugh to realise this was a loaded comment.

'Relaxation techniques, for instance,' she persisted doggedly.

'You do seem tense,' he agreed.

Kat gritted her teeth. 'I'm perfectly relaxed!' she yelled.

'Of course you are.'

'I'm willing to be reasonably flexible up to a point. I expected that, living in, but I can't possibly be on call twenty-four hours.'

'Why? Is there some boyfriend in the background who gets stroppy if you neglect him...or family commitments...?'

Her expression darkened. 'There's nobody,' she said flatly.

Matt's eyes narrowed. He recognised no-go signs when he saw them. Was Kathleen running away from a disastrous love affair...?

'Then where's the problem?' His tone implied she was unreasonably creating problems where there weren't any. 'Good. That's settled.'

'I didn't agree to anything.'

'But you will do after a bit more fencing. I'm just saving time. Incidentally, you were wanting to assess my capabilities...'

Puzzled by the reference, she nodded.

'Most people think I'm capable of anything.' He grinned down into her startled face, picked up a cake off the plate and crammed it whole into his mouth. He jammed open the door with a crutch.

Matt raised his voice. 'Send Miss Macdonald and Mr Smith into the library, will you, Mrs Nichols?'

On cue the doorbell rang.

I wonder how he does that?

'And, Mrs Nichols, will you have my things moved again? Miss Wray thinks I should sleep downstairs.' He turned back to Kat. '*Satisfied?*'

Kat refused to be thawed by the charm in his smile. The memory of how it had felt when he'd forced her down on her knees beside him kept popping into her head at the most inconvenient moments; this resulted in her nervous system being in a constant state of painful alert. She pursed her lips in disapproval.

'You should be resting, not entertaining.'

'This is business, not pleasure.'

'That's even worse!' she exclaimed in an appalled voice. 'You should be taking things easy.'

Matt gave a long-suffering sigh. 'Try and keep your maternal inclinations under control, Kathleen,' he advised in a bored drawl.

Kat gave a gasp of outrage and went bright red. Her hands curled into small fists; the awful man had as good as called her *mumsy*.

'I can assure you,' she choked, 'that I don't feel even *vaguely* maternal towards you!'

Matt's wicked grin flashed out. 'I thought not, but it's nice to have it confirmed.'

Kat was left to massage the stiff muscles of her neck, and think wistful thoughts about hospitals, boring routine, and patients who hadn't started shaving!

CHAPTER THREE

LATER that evening, Kat was sitting reading—or at least *trying* to read—in her room when there was a discreet knock on her door.

She got up off the bed and almost guiltily smoothed the quilt. 'Come in,' she called self-consciously.

The housekeeper appeared. She smiled in a friendly way at Kat.

'I was just wondering, miss, if you'd like a tray in your room? I'm going to have my supper in the kitchen. You can join me…?'

Kat gave a sigh of relief. She'd needn't have worried that she'd be expected to dine with Matt.

'Please, it's Kat…' She smiled warmly at the older woman.

She was glad now that she hadn't given in to the foolish, vain impulse of changing into something less functional on the off-chance that she'd be summoned to provide a sparkling dinner companion for Matt. I'm the hired help, and, she told herself stoutly, glad of it!

What girl with an ounce of sense would want to dress up in a skimpy frock and sit across from the most scandalously good-looking man in the world?

'I'd like that—to eat with you, that is. I was beginning to feel a bit lonesome.' This seemed the time to come clean. 'To tell you the truth, I'm not really up to speed with this upstairs-downstairs stuff.' She wrinkled her small straight nose and gave a rueful smile.

'Oh, don't worry, my dear,' the older woman responded, leading the way down the well-lit hallway. 'You mustn't feel you have to stay in your room. We're not at all grand here…'

That rather depends, Kat thought, responding to this soothing news with a strained smile, on what you're used to.

'That's the way Mrs Devlin likes it. There's only me and Mr Edwards, a couple of girls who come in from the village and the gardeners. Mrs Devlin is very fond of her garden. Cook's retired; she has a cottage in the grounds, but she always comes in if we've got guests; she wouldn't like it if we got anyone else.'

'Yes, the garden's very beautiful.' Kat cleared her throat. 'I was wondering,' she began casually—it would never do for anyone to realise she felt the urgent need of a chaperon, 'will Drusilla—Mrs Devlin—will she be home tonight?'

The housekeeper led the way down the wide shallow staircase. 'I shouldn't think so,' she called over her shoulder. 'Mrs Devlin always gives us plenty of notice if she intends to stay with us.'

Kat's knuckles whitened against the graceful curve of the banister. 'But I thought…' Kat, aware that the other woman, who was waiting for her to catch up, had begun look at her with a curious expression, forced herself to relax. 'I thought this was her house.'

'Well, it is…at least on paper, though of course it was Mr Devlin senior who was brought up here,' she explained chattily. She gave a furtive glance over her shoulder as if to confirm there was nobody lurking in the corners with a recording device. 'I think it was for tax reasons he had it put in Mrs Devlin's name,' she hissed with conspiratorial candour.

'So Mrs Devlin doesn't live here herself.' It seemed incomprehensible to Kat that anyone could keep a big, fully staffed house like this one empty.

'Heavens, no. They live in the Castle.'

Of course, the Castle… *Where else?* Kat gave a sick-looking smile. I've been lulled here under false pretences, she thought indignantly!

She was working in luxurious surroundings, for a man who was the stuff female fantasies were made of, and she was being paid a small fortune for doing so! Her plight was going to elicit her a lot of sympathy!

For the first time she started to think Matt's more fanciful notions about his mother might not be entirely the result of a fevered imagination.

'They used to spend most of the school holidays here when young Mr Matthew was a boy. Mrs Devlin had a strict rule—no business talk, she used to say. I don't know what she'd make of that.' The housekeeper gave a snort of disapproval and glanced towards the closed oak-panelled door; they were passing the library as she spoke.

'Mr Devlin is still…?'

The older woman nodded.

Kat clicked her tongue in exasperation. God, but that man had the sense of a sparrow on a suicide mission, she thought angrily!

'They've been in there the whole evening. He asked for sandwiches to be sent in. Cook was most put out, I can tell you.' Kat began to feel uneasy that they'd not progressed past the offending door. 'He looks dead on his feet.'

'He does?' The way the housekeeper was looking at her made the sinking feeling in her stomach get worse.

'I'd get short shrift if *I* tried to tell him.'

'He wouldn't listen to me!' Kat protested weakly.

'You're *medical*.' The housekeeper produced what she obviously felt to be her trump card.

Kat gave a sigh and resigned herself to the inevitable. She resented being placed in this position; she hadn't come here to be a nursemaid. Her anger was aimed at Matt, not the housekeeper.

Since when did helicopter pilots hold business meetings that went on for hours, anyhow? she wondered, squaring her shoulders and raising her clenched fist to the door. Perhaps it was more of a social occasion she was about to try and throw cold water on…? Well, so be it; the man should know better.

She knocked and strode confidently into the room—those years shifting scenery at the amateur dramatics hadn't been wasted after all.

This was a library in the real sense, not a couple of flat-pack bookshelves and a stack of paperbacks. She had never known anyone who owned his very own library before, and even if this wasn't strictly Matt Devlin's he looked quite comfortable in the role. He also looked, as Mrs Nichols had indicated, dead on his feet, or rather not his feet—fortunately even his stupidity had limits.

His face was turned away from her but even from where she was standing she could see the dark shadows beneath his eyes that contrasted dramatically with his stark pallor. Kat experienced two wildly conflicting desires—one was to batter some sense into his thick skull, the other to wrap him up in cotton wool and protect him from every little draught.

He was seated in a leather swivel chair with a high buttoned back. There was a laptop open on the big mahogany desk and piles of papers were spread over the gleaming surface. Matt and two people, one male and one female, standing either side of him, appeared to be poring over them. He still hadn't looked up.

'Tell Cook the sandwiches were delicious.' Kat watched him slyly shift a sheaf of papers to disguise the fact the plate was barely touched before he lifted his head. His engaging smile looked a bit frayed around the edges.

When he saw who was standing there, shock and something else, something that made Kat's responsive stomach muscles quiver, widened his deep blue eyes.

'Kathleen!' The line bisecting his dark eyebrows deepened suspiciously. 'What are you doing here?' He drew a tired hand through his dark hair.

'Saving you from yourself,' she told him grimly.

Matt blinked. 'Was that in the contract?' he enquired mildly.

A paper drifted from the top of a pile and Kat automatically reached out and caught it. She barely glanced at the typed sheet but the familiar eye-catching logo on the letterhead was hard to miss—she'd flown Fair Flights on her last trip abroad. This innocuous detail alone wouldn't have made her hand tremble as she replaced it, but the bold signature below the printed title of managing director did!

'Thank you.'

Not a pilot—he ran the whole damned thing! Kat stood there feeling incredibly stupid for not catching on earlier; there had been enough clues! Boss of a firm that had flouted all the rules and succeeded—the role fitted this man like a glove.

'You'd know all about contracts, I suppose,' Kat accused.

If Matt was surprised by her comment or the spark of anger in her eyes, he hid it well.

'It's all in the detail,' he agreed equably.

'For a supposedly clever man,' she snapped, 'you can be remarkably stupid at times.' Well, I was wondering what I was going to say—now I know.

The noise of the guests' collective jaws gaping was almost audible; even Matt, whom she knew wasn't easy to shock, looked startled this time.

Please be startled amused not startled mad, she prayed.

Without taking his eyes from her defiant face, he pushed his chair backwards; the castors moved silently over the dense carpet.

'Grace, Tim, I don't think you've met Kathleen.'

'Nice to meet you,' the young man with the receding hairline and the horn-rimmed specs said respectfully.

The woman just looked through her heavily made-up eyes and then, with jangle of earrings and a confident little smile that dismissed Kat in her dowdy unimaginative clothes as no competition at all, returned her attention to Matt.

Kat let her own lips twitch but stopped just sort of smiling. She didn't dislike all women who were almost six foot and a size ten on principle, but she felt that on this occasion she was willing to make an exception.

'I'm sorry to disturb you, Mr Devlin, but you should be in bed.'

Kat watched his eyes narrow and felt sure all hell was about to break loose. He was going to remind her in front of the interested audience just who was boss.

Just because he didn't yell straight off, I had to go and get cocky.

It took several seconds of squinting before Matt's blurry vision cleared. He saw that the magnificent and irritating Miss Wray was looking apprehensive but unrepentant. He couldn't help but admire her sheer guts.

'Is this desire to get me in bed a personal—' he let the thought hang in the air '—or professional request, Kathleen?'

She blushed, even though Matt didn't look capable of seducing anyone right now. Her concern deepened; he looked like a man whose adrenaline levels were dropping rapidly. The over-stimulated brightness she'd seen in his eyes when she'd entered the room was fast becoming a glazed vagueness.

'I really must get on top of that over-developed mothering instinct of mine.'

'Touché!' He turned to his silent acolytes. 'I know what you're thinking…bolshy, pushy…'

'You forgot to add correct.'

He shot her an impatient frown. 'I didn't forget,

Kathleen, I was rudely interrupted. As I was about to say, unfortunately just now she's also right. *Satisfied?*'

Satisfaction was not the emotion uppermost in Kat's mind as she folded her arms across her chest.

'I rather lose track of time,' he conceded. 'The fact is, folks, I've felt more alert in my sleep.'

'Right, boss, no problem.' The spectacles responded immediately. He went to help Matt as he pulled himself to his feet and then very obviously thought better of it—Kat thought he'd made the right decision.

The woman waited until he was on his feet before reaching up and placing a kiss on his cheek. 'Of course, Matt. You should have said.'

Kat could almost see the redhead wondering what she'd missed the first time as she subjected her to a second unfriendly scrutiny.

'Can I help…?'

'Thank you, Grace, but that's what Kat is paid to do—aren't you, Kathleen.'

She heard the slight slur in his voice and looked sharply into his eyes. She recognised with some alarm that he was a lot nearer to total exhaustion than she had imagined.

'Paid obscenely well,' she agreed, surreptitiously shadowing his slow progress across the room.

'I didn't know you'd employed a nurse,' the redhead exclaimed.

Matt's deep drowning blue eyes were fixed on Kat's face. 'I haven't.'

Kat felt sure it wasn't by chance he didn't enlighten them further. Whether this was because he didn't explain himself on principle or he enjoyed embarrassing her, Kat couldn't decide.

Five minutes later—which had seemed a lot longer at times to Kat—Matt reached above his head and pulled a pillow from the pile at the bedhead. Wearily, he shoved it under his neck.

His big body was slewed at an awkward angle, half on and half off the bed, but Kat—who had thought she'd have to call for reinforcements at one point during their transfer—was relieved they'd made it this far. She watched his eyes close, as if the effort of grabbing the pillow had exhausted his last resources.

'I feel drunk, and I've not touched a drop,' he informed her in a puzzled accent.

The dark veil of his thick lashes cast a dark shadow against his high cheekbones. It would have been a massive exaggeration to say he looked vulnerable, but in repose his face looked a lot softer. Kat, in danger of succumbing to dangerous mushy feelings, pulled her eyes away from his face.

'It's sleep deprivation,' she informed him tartly. 'You can only cheat your body so long; even *you* have to sleep eventually. And actually I'm not *paid* to do this,' she added in a disgruntled undertone.

'Do what?' Matt didn't open his eyes.

Kat slid off his remaining shoe and, with a bit of huffing, succeeded in swinging his long legs onto the bed on which he was lying.

'I'm not paid to put you to bed.'

She pulled the thin cover up over his still clothed body; there was no way she was removing anything but his shoes. She tucked the cover under his chin.

'You did it out of the goodness of your heart.'

His warm breath brushed her cheek as she straightened up. 'I'm missing my supper for this. I must be mad!'

'Not mad, sweet.' Then he went and spoilt it by adding in a silkily stagy drawl that robbed his words of sincerity, 'I'm touched by such a selfless gesture in this avaricious old world.'

'Will you be serious for a minute?' she pleaded tightly.

Matt's heavy eyelids lifted for a moment, and she could almost feel the enormous effort the gesture cost him. 'For you, anything,' he said before they sleepily closed.

'It's important you ease yourself gently back into work,' she told him worriedly.

'I know, I know...' He yawned and lifted a hand over his head. 'I just tend to be a bit over-protective of my baby...'

There was no mistaking the proprietorial note in his rueful voice.

'Your *baby!* You mean you don't just run the airline, you own it?' Kat was startled into exclaiming.

'Well at the beginning there were two of us, until good old *reliable* Damon very nearly gambled our assets out from under us.'

'Gambled?' Kat ejaculated. 'It's not possible.'

'Want to bet?' Matt challenged, grinning at his own wit. 'It's a solo show these days,' he told her, his deep voice slurred and sleepy.

Almost before he had finished speaking, the rhythm of his breathing had altered.

She stood there listening to the deep, even rhythm for a few moments. Ironically they did have something in common after all; they'd both been the innocent victims of a gambling addiction.

'Shut up and go to sleep,' she advised, determined that for once she'd get the last word.

It seemed an invasion of his privacy somehow to stand there gawking, but there was something about his face that fascinated Kat. She jumped guiltily when he murmured sleepily and flung an arm over his head. The covers slid down and she couldn't help but notice how tight his shirt pulled against his neck.

How would I feel if he choked to death in the night just because I was too squeamish to loosen his buttons? She fought to subdue her overpowering reluctance to touch him.

With a wildly beating heart, she sat on the edge of the bed and reached over to loosen the top button, which due to her shaking fingers wasn't as easy as it sounded, and then the next.

His skin was warm… Kat expelled her breath in an angry gusty sigh. Well, what did you expect, idiot? she asked herself sarcastically. The man's not made of marble!

No, he was made of flesh and blood and other intriguing things that the modest sliver of flesh she'd revealed gave tantalising hints of. Intriguing things like firm muscles and dark curling body hair. Under her fingers she could feel the steady rise and fall of his chest.

'That should do it,' she announced to nobody in particular.

Still she still didn't move.

Where would be the harm?

She only had to stretch her fingers a little wider and she'd be able to feel… Beads of moisture broke out over her upper lip. It was only when her fingertips began to quiver that the full shame of what she'd been contemplating hit her.

Choking back a cry of shamed horror, she backed out of the room.

CHAPTER FOUR

IF SHE'D expected Matt to sleep the clock around Kat was disappointed—or maybe not. It was the maybe not part that bothered her! Anyone would think she was anxious to see him.

The message relayed by Mrs Nichols during breakfast was that he'd like to see her in the pool in forty-five minutes. That had happened forty-eight minutes ago, according to her watch.

Despite the fact she was beginning to feel a little too warm in the baggy tee-shirt that she wore over her swimsuit, Kat felt strangely reluctant to strip off. Instead she sat at the side of the pool and trailed her toes in the water.

She was indulging in a little childish splashing when Matt emerged from the door that connected with his bedroom suite. She'd already kind of admitted to herself that Matt Devlin gave off sexual vibes of an earthy raw variety to which she wasn't *totally* invulnerable—after last night, did she have a choice?—so she expected to feel something...only not this much *something!*

Despite the humidified constant temperature in the poolhouse a rash of goose bumps spontaneously broke out over her skin as he appeared. Every step he took nearer seemed to trigger a new body system to go haywire... The complete disintegration of her nervous system didn't take long at all.

Anyone would think you'd never seen a man in pair of swimming shorts before...! Pull yourself together, Kat! Under the cover of retying her ponytail she gave herself a sharp lecture on the evils of behaving with all the discrimination of a groupie!

She gave her blonde hair an extra vicious tweak just

before discovering, much to her horror, that good intentions and determination didn't come into the equation. She was suffering from a *visceral* response over which she apparently had no control... The only alternative left open to her seemed to be to treat it like bad case of the flu and wait for her immunity to develop a few defences—for the sake of her sanity and self-respect, sooner would be better than later!

He had discarded the crutches in favour of a single cane. Small wonder his mother wanted someone around to keep an eye on him; left to himself, the man would probably run a marathon within the month!

She continued to watch his slow but determined progress with a hammering heart and an expression she hoped and prayed was unimpeachably objective. Ironically, considering his halting progress, his was a body built for speed, long lean and sleekly muscular, with no suggestion of bulk about the well-defined slabs of tight muscle. It would take more than a leg held together by a selection of nuts and bolts to alter the fact that this man had a raw earthy magnetism right off the scale!

Her stomach a riot of butterflies, she got to her feet just before he reached the shallow flight of steps that led into the pool. A thick uncomfortable silence fell as their eyes eventually collided. Her own showed a worrying tendency to cling to his strong lean face.

'Seen enough...?'

For a moment she went rigid with shock; then it slowly dawned on her that it hadn't been an accusation. She could have wept with relief.

How convenient that she had a legitimate reason to look at his body. It was part of her role. *A tough job but somebody had to do it!*

'You've kept your muscle tone very well—' she told him in a cool tone that suggested her scrutiny had been completely clinical '—considering,' she finished weakly.

'Considering I'm as weak as a kitten.' He glanced down with impatience at a body which had once responded obediently to every demand, no matter how harsh, he made of it.

'*Considering* the long-term bed-rest, traction and sundry restrictions you've endured,' she corrected him firmly. 'Actually, I'm impressed,' she admitted lightly. Just how impressed was something she was going to keep to herself. 'I was expecting it to be much worse.'

He laid the ebony-topped cane down. For a second she thought he was going to ignore the arm she automatically held out for his support. The wry smile that twitched the corners of his mouth didn't touch the bleak aspect of his blue eyes as his arm came down to rest lightly on her forearm.

The cool dryness of his flesh contrasted with the sticky heat of her own. A sliver of sexual awareness sliced through her; the neat concoction combined with his proximity spooked her so badly it was hard not to follow her gut instinct and turn tail. This was sexual attraction on a scale she'd not encountered before.

'You make it sound as though I ought to be grateful.'

Ignoring the solid lump of panic lodged behind her breastbone, Kat smiled. 'I'm already over my permitted number of platitudes for one day,' she retorted drily.

'You've got a limit?' His eyes widened with mock shock. 'That makes you a very unusual angel of mercy.'

'I bet you gave the nursing staff hell!' she accused huskily. And I bet they came running back for more!

The devilish glint in his eyes intensified. 'A man's got to do something to amuse himself when he's stuck in bed all day,' he confessed, displaying no signs of remorse for his alleged behaviour.

It made Kat's blood run cold—which, on sober reflection, was probably better than a constant simmer—to imagine him amusing himself at her expense. A woman, who swore she hated him, being turned into a mass of seething hormones by his bad blue eyes? With his twisted sense of humour, he'd never be able to resist a joke like that!

'You look a lot better than you did last night.' In retrospect, she wondered whether it had been such a good idea—in the interest of peace and harmony—to have brought up the subject of the previous night. She wasn't sure he was the sort of man who'd like anyone to see him with his defences down.

'Ah, last night; I wondered how long you could resist saying, "I told you so"?'

'I was just making an observation. I'm sure you already realise how stupid you were being yesterday without me rubbing it in.'

Kat already regretted letting her sharp tongue run away with her, but much to her surprise Matt didn't seem to mind; there was an amused, almost appreciative gleam in his eyes.

'I'm only just realising what a soul of restraint you are, Kathleen.'

Their eyes clashed and suddenly the humour fizzled away, leaving an almost electrical charge in its place. Kat was the first to look away.

'Hold on a minute,' she requested curtly, pulling one arm elbow-first out of the oversized tee-shirt. 'Grab on there,' she suggested, indicating her free shoulder with her chin, 'while I get this off.' A quick wriggle and it was over her head.

Matt expelled his breath in long luxurious sigh. It hardly mattered that this was no skin fest; he hadn't been this close to a skimpily clad female for some time. The racing-backed swimsuit she wore was black, the unadorned high-necked type that competitive female swimmers wore to flatten their natural buoyancy aids in the hope it would shave a few micros of a second off their times.

Even accounting for the design factor and reinforced Lycra, there was no disguising the fact Kat had a knock-out figure; from whichever angle you looked at her there was no mistaking she was *all* female! There would be absolutely no chance of a man grazing himself on her hipbones—a bloke got tired sometimes of females trying to starve their curves into submission.

The sound of her clearing her throat noisily brought his eyes reluctantly from softly rounded thigh level to her pink-cheeked, predictably indignant face. The clear grey eyes were spitting sparks and her cute nose was twitching with temper.

'Shall I give you a twirl, or have you seen enough?'

He saw no harm in playing out the moral degenerate card—her opinion of him couldn't get much lower—not if the expression in her eyes was any indicator.

'Have you ever considered a bikini? The skimpy sort?' he mused, elaborating with some pleasure on the theme, 'Triangles tied together...'

She snorted and did that flouncy cross thing with her head and her ponytail smacked her in the eye... One eye watering, she blinked rapidly and took an angry step away from him. Being an observant man, he noticed the bounciness extended to other areas.

This awakening sexual interest was probably a sign that he was getting back to normal. As Kathleen had a habit of saying...it was nothing personal. Nice try, mate, but just who are you kidding? Not himself, that was for sure—not with a piece of self-deception that flagrant!

'I was just being a dutiful friend. Joe will expect a full report...I take it you did notice my *heterosexual* friend, Joe, was deeply smitten?'

'Don't be daft...'

Actually, Joe fell in and out of love at regular intervals, so Matt wasn't reading too much into it. The thought that maybe Joe wasn't the only one a little smitten occurred, only to be speedily dismissed. If a bit of mild flirtation

would make his convalescence any less tedious, where was
the harm? The girl had made herself a legitimate target the
moment she'd announced he left her cold...a blatant
lie...and she'd only have herself to blame if he made her
eat her words.

Would she recognise Joe if she met him in the street?
Kat was ashamed to acknowledge she couldn't be sure. It
was all Matt's fault; he was the sort of man that tended to
be the cynosure of attention without even trying. The Joes
of this world, worthy and *nice* to a man, faded into insig-
nificance; there was no justice. God, I'm so shallow!

'And don't blame poor Joe for your lecherous tenden-
cies!' she advised contemptuously. Riding high on a wave
of moral superiority, she blithely ignored the jarring note
of hypocrisy in her comment.

After all, she reasoned, the circumstances were totally
different. Matt had not been around scantily clad females
for some time, so you couldn't really take his interest personally, whereas she didn't stare hungrily at just *any* man!

A distracted dreamy expression flitted across her disapproving features... He *had* looked hungry... Recalling that
hard *male* expression made her stomach muscles spasm
painfully.

'*Poor* Joe?' He clicked his tongue. 'That doesn't sound
promising.'

His laughter, low and effortlessly sexy, was a wake-up
call for a dreamy Kat. When he'd looked at her like *that*
he'd just been responding in the preconditioned male response to weigh up any female that came within ogling
distance. It was no more complicated than the blinking re-
flex. Men were pretty primitive creatures when you came
right down to it!

Be realistic! Why would *he*—her eyes swept resentfully
up the length of his long, lean, spectacular body—look at
me?

Kat had few illusions about her figure. The hour-glass

shape might have excited admiration during an era less fixated by androgynous slenderness, but by today's standards she knew she would be considered positively gross by the purist. She'd decided a long time ago she wasn't about to punish and starve her body to sculpt it to fit in with some media-hyped ideal.

'I feel sure that Joe would appreciate your efforts on his behalf, but shall we get back to what we're actually here for?' Matt conceded her point with a shrug. 'Actually, I don't think you can have been so bad a patient as you make out. It wasn't luck that kept your muscle tone; you must have been pretty diligent about your exercises.'

'I live to work my quadriceps,' he agreed drily. 'That's why I opted for pool work this morning. Hydrotherapy has a slightly lower tedium quotient. You don't have a problem with that, do you?'

'Not at all; it's a good idea. Though I'm not used to working in anything this…big.' She finished lamely.

It was pointless trying to explain to anyone who found it normal to have an Olympic-sized swimming pool that she found the opulence of her surroundings slightly intimidating.

'You probably find it difficult to believe, but I used to be in pretty good shape.'

Used to be! Was he serious? As far as Kat could tell, he still was—and then some!

Broad, powerful shoulders, washboard flat belly and snaky slim hips attached to long, *long* legs. His skin tones were naturally dark, but they still seemed pale in contrast to the dark body hair sprinkled across his broad chest. Her eyes dropped compulsively to the thin arrow of dark hair that disappeared under the waistband of his swimming trunks and her wayward stomach did a treble flip.

'I know you're in a hurry, but it's all about realistic goals.'

Now that's something you should remember, Kat, she

told herself firmly. Men like Matt Devlin were not 'realistic goals' for girls like her; he was the type to give a girl a good time—probably a *very* good time—and disappear into the sunset.

'Your idea of realistic, or mine?'

Kat could sympathise with his barely restrained restless impatience.

'I'd suggest a compromise if I thought you understood the meaning of the word,' she came back acerbically.

He grinned down at her through wolfish gritted teeth. 'You've got entirely the wrong idea, Baby-face. Concession is my middle name...'

'Baby-face...?' She grimaced. *'Please.'*

'It just sort of slipped out.'

'I think I feel deeply insulted that you look at me and automatically think *Baby-face*. Unless, that is, you call all females ''Baby-face''?'

He wondered what she'd do if he told her what he did think when he looked at her. For one brief, insane moment he even toyed with the idea of finding out, then common sense prevailed.

'Not so far.' Head on one side, he appeared to give the notion some thought. 'But I don't think many of them would have minded...outside the work environment, naturally. I'm strictly PC at work.'

'I don't think all that much of the women you know,' she sniffed scornfully, thinking of the slinky redhead.

'You and Drusilla in perfect harmony once more.'

'I hardly know your mother.' And taking everything this virtual stranger had told her—or more specifically *not* told her—as the gospel truth had got her where she was now.

He zeroed in on what seemed like a whopping great inconsistency. 'What happened to the old family friend thing?'

Kat gave an exasperated sigh. He had to be the most suspicious person she'd ever come across, but then she supposed he had his reasons for being suspicious. The more she thought about it, the more likely it seemed to Kat that, for reasons which remained a mystery, Drusilla had been trying to set her up with her millionaire son.

'Like I told you, she went to school with Mum, but they lost contact years ago. They met up again relatively recently.'

Drusilla had been opening a new pain control clinic at the local hospital and Kat's mother had been one of the first patients.

'When are you expecting your mother?' When Drusilla did turn up Kat was going to do some straight talking; she thought she was due an explanation! Why, anything could have happened, she brooded resentfully... I could have fallen in love with the man!

'What makes you think I am expecting her? Did she say she'd be here?'

Kat was quite relieved when his sharp interrogative tone wrenched her away from her uncomfortable introspection.

'Not *exactly*,' she admitted. Eyes narrowed slightly, she reviewed their last conversation. 'But she did give the impression...'

'Yes, she's quite good at doing that.'

'I'd noticed.' Kat couldn't help sounding bitter.

'*Interesting!*' One dark brow quirked as he contemplated the angry pink spots on her smooth cheeks. 'Just how much do you know about the family situation?'

'Family situation?' she echoed airily, giving a passable imitation of not knowing what he was talking about...and furthermore not being interested.

'Unless it's relevant to your treatment there's absolutely no need for me to—'

'Like you're not the least little bit curious...!'

His laconic drawl really got under her skin. 'Well, of course I am! Who wouldn't be when you've just implied there's some juicy secret?'

'Fair point.'

Kat blinked. She was beginning to recognise a sort of pattern; every time she was spoiling for a fight, he threw her off balance completely by turning all reasonable.

'You know who my father is?'

She could tell by the way he said it that he took her affirmation as read.

'Should I?'

Matt looked shocked, and then frankly sceptical of her reply.

'You're joking?'

It wasn't until the last few years that people had stopped referring to him as Connor Devlin's son—God, at one point Matt had even considered having his name changed by deed poll! He'd worked hard to establish himself as his own person, not a shadowy version of the old man, for so long it was vaguely disorientating to discover someone who didn't know who the great man was!

'No I'm not joking; neither am I being being evasive. Unlike some people I could mention,' she reflected with a bitter aside. 'Actually, I didn't even know you had a father.'

'You weren't very well briefed, were you?'

'You don't know the half of it,' Kat responded with feeling. 'Your mother told me you were a helicopter pilot.'

'I am.'

'That's the clever part,' Kat reflected darkly, unable to take her eyes off the sculpted muscles of his midriff.

'My God!' Matt breathed in a shaken tone. 'You mean it! You really didn't know...'

Kat wrenched her eyes back to eye level; the change of scenery offered very little relief for her lust-transfixed thoughts.

'Oh, it gets better,' she told him bitterly. 'I even thought she was paying my salary because you couldn't afford to. How funny is that? I thought she lived here. Now I find out you are rich!'

'Is that a problem—the rich part, not the stupid part?'

Kat dealt him a withering look. 'I don't care about your money…!'

Matt found that against all the odds he believed her.

'I care about being lied to.'

He heard the emotional quiver in her voice and the amusement died from his eyes; he knew all about being lied to. He still continued to look at her with an expression of unholy fascination.

'Perhaps we should teach my meddling mother a lesson.'

His silky, soothing tone sent a sliver of apprehension down her spine.

'When she does turn up to see how her machinations are going, we could let her think her plan worked.'

'How could we do that?'

'We could pretend to be madly in love.'

Pretend to be in love? Kissing and touching—wouldn't they be almost obligatory under such circumstances? On one level, she found the idea exciting in a wild reckless sort of way. Another part of her instinctively knew that she couldn't settle for make-believe.

Kat drew a deep sustaining breath as it hit her with the force of a tidal wave—*I wouldn't be pretending.*

'It would probably cure her of matchmaking for good.'

'Rough justice—how poetic. You're just as warped and manipulative as she is!' she accused shakily. She felt as if the truth were written all over her face.

Matt shrugged. 'It was just a thought.'

'Do me a favour. Don't think.' She took a deep breath and changed the subject. 'You were giving me the low-down on your father. If I'd thought about him at all, I suppose I'd assumed he was dead.'

For some reason this last comment seemed to amuse Matt the most.

'No, he's very much alive,' he told her gravely. 'With

an emphasis on the *very*. He's very fond of mentioning he's got more energy than a man half his age.'

'Would that younger man be you?'

'Give the lady a prize.'

'You don't get on with him...?'

'Go straight to the top of the class. My father and I haven't communicated for several years; he's disinherited me.'

'And I take it there's a lot to disinherit you from...?' she prompted. A person just couldn't start a story and leave it like that.

'You've heard of Atlantica Airlines?'

Kat nodded. 'Of course.'

'That's my father.'

Her eyes widened. *'Gosh!'* She looked around their surroundings, realising now why he took such opulence for granted. 'Then you set up in...'

'Competition.' He inclined his dark head. 'That's right. He wanted me to do the dutiful son thing and learn at the master's feet.'

'I can see how that might cause a bit of friction. But surely after the accident...?' she exclaimed, unable to comprehend the sort of paternal animosity that could survive this life-threatening crisis. 'I didn't mean to pry,' she added uncomfortably.

Matt's massive muscle-packed shoulders lifted, and Kat, to whom the mechanics of muscle and sinew were no mystery, found herself momentarily distracted by this simple action... This is getting silly, she told herself angrily.

'It's no secret,' he told her. 'It's the old nurturing a snake in his bosom story. He's considered me a traitor from the day I became the opposition. So, you see, you've got caught up in a long-running family feud. Mum never gives up on the idea of a big reconciliation. She's got this master plan, you see, to get Dad and I back together.'

'That's got nothing to do with me...'

Matt shook his head slowly. Now that they were both officially victims of Drusilla he seemed inclined to view her in an almost sympathetic manner.

'Me producing a son is meant to reduce the old man to a sentimental push-over...'

Privately, going on the information she had, Kat thought such an event was highly unlikely, given the two men involved both seemed extraordinarily obstinate and inflexible.

One dark brow lifted. 'That's where you come in...'

'Me...?' she echoed innocently.

'I can't produce a son alone...'

'Does it have to be a boy?'

'No,' he conceded, 'just a Devlin. Well, half-Devlin...the other half.'

Kat's eyes widened to saucer-size. 'She picked me for my child-bearing hips?'

'Don't panic. I think she's backing a loser, too.'

Kat couldn't decide if this was a direct indictment of her hips or her overall appeal—or lack of it. Either way, it was hard to stand there and act as if you didn't care when the man you were potty about casually dismissed you as a possible mate.

'Poor Drusilla!' Putting aside her unhappy personal involvement, she couldn't help but feel for the other woman.

It was the ultimate divided loyalties scenario. Caught between a husband and son. Kat couldn't imagine many situations she'd like less.

'It must be hard for her. Does your father know you're staying here?'

'Probably,' Matt conceded carelessly.

Kat noticed he had the same closed expression on his face every time he mentioned his father.

'They've come to some sort of compromise—that they don't discuss me—but I'm sure he knows what she's up to.'

'I thought my family was odd...' A cloud passed over

her face as it struck her afresh that she no longer had a family, odd or otherwise.

Her tactlessness amused him; the shadow in her eyes intrigued him. 'Perhaps we could exchange odd anecdotes, some time…?'

Kat didn't respond to his smile. 'Perhaps,' she said, confident that she'd never feel inclined to confide her family secrets to this man. She moved down the wide shallow steps until her ankles were covered by water. When she lifted her head she found her eyes were on a level with the scars on his left leg.

A naturally empathic person, Kat had been forced over the years to build up the necessary defences against other people's suffering. She'd learnt that she couldn't identify personally with someone's pain without it affecting her work. But one glance at the surgeon's clever handiwork here and those rudimentary defences were stripped clean away. She stood there, feeling emotions so raw they hurt.

'Want a guided tour of the scar sites?'

Only a total deviant could have found the invitation erotic. Kat lowered her troubled gaze, feeling deeply ashamed.

He touched the one above his knee. 'This is from the external fixation. When that got infected, they eventually opted for the internal metalwork.' He traced a vertical line. 'Quite a mess.'

Kat had this crazy explosive image in her head of tracing the fading line with her fingers…her lips. Her entire body was shaken by a hot shiver.

'I've seen worse,' she croaked. 'Here, let me help you into the water.' Pity it's not cold—I could do with it!

'Give it to me from the female angle.'

'*Female angle?*'

'You know what I mean. What is your gut reaction?' he elaborated casually. 'Pity, distaste, revulsion…? Don't pull your punches. I'd like to know what to expect.'

Kat shook her head in disbelief. 'You know, the vanity of men never ceases to amaze me,' she marvelled angrily. 'You think women are *that* shallow?'

'Now that you come to mention it...' Ignoring her extended hand, he manoeuvred himself down the first couple of steps pretty slickly. From what she could see, Kat didn't think he'd need her services for too long.

Kat wished she'd concentrated harder when Drusilla had been explaining about some girlfriend—or had it been a fiancée?—who had dumped Matt because she had panicked at the idea of disfigurement. Silly fool, Kat thought, intensely scornful of this fickle airhead... If you loved someone, what did a few scars matter?

'Just because you've had a bad experience...' She immediately sensed the wary aggression in his tense stance. 'Drusilla mentioned a girl...' she admitted with a brief conciliatory grin. Her bosom swelled with indignation. 'She didn't sound very...*nice*,' she sniffed.

'Not nice, but very naughty,' Matt told her with a nostalgic gleam in his eyes. He hadn't expected or wanted Angela to hang around when the going got tough; they hadn't had that sort of relationship.

Kat, her stomach churning queasily, didn't want to think about what sort of behaviour *naughty* covered. Neither was she totally convinced by the fact he was displaying none of the classical symptoms of rejection. Pride would never permit him to admit that he'd been hurt... Maybe he was trying to play down the incident deliberately? Perhaps he was genuinely seeking reassurance...? Part of her ached to provide that reassurance; part of her ached to give him whatever he wanted!

Looking at his hard, almost painfully handsome face, Kat found it hard to believe the latter could be true. He had to be the most confident person she'd ever come across. Appearances could be deceptive, she reminded herself. Maybe the ego thing was a cover-up.

Just when she felt inclined to give him the benefit of the doubt and her concern for his emotional welfare had risen accordingly he went and spoilt it with a scornful, 'If I wanted *nice* I'd buy a dog.'

'Niceness and fidelity don't seem to feature very high on your list of virtues,' she observed tartly as she backed down the steps.

It was fortunate monitoring his progress was part of her job because Kat didn't think she could have torn her eyes from him if her life had depended on it!

'I take it they do on yours?' He gave a sigh of pleasure as the warm water closed about his waist.

'Well, I haven't lost hope of finding someone who can see beyond a D-cup, someone who loves me for more than my body.'

A very worrying expression had slid into his eyes when she'd mentioned D-cup. It occurred to her she was in danger of exacerbating an already tense situation!

'Let's try this first, shall we...?' She began to demonstrate a few gentle exercises which Matt immediately copied. After a few moments, she was satisfied he was more than up to the task.

'And will you love him—this *paragon*.' Matt continued their conversation as if nothing had been said in the interim, and the contemptuous curl of his lip spoilt the gentle rhythm Kat had built up '—for more than his body?' Loving her body wouldn't be too onerous a task for most men.

She could hardly beg him to avoid the L subject without inviting unwelcome speculation. What was she meant to say...? *I've fallen madly, deeply, dangerously in love with you, so please don't bring up the subject?*

'Did you see me falling about in revulsion at your scars?'

'That's not the same. You don't fancy me...' Was it her guilty conscience that imbued his tone with scepticism? 'You don't even like me, or have you forgotten?'

'I haven't forgotten!' she retorted, her bosom heaving as

though she'd just sprinted several lengths of the pool. 'And I'm not likely to while you continue to go out of your way to be objectionable. Shall we take a break?'

'So soon?' The ends of his hair were wet; when he shook his head the excess moisture transferred itself to his mocking face. 'I don't think your fitness levels are what they should be.'

This not-so-veiled reference to her breathless discomposed state brought an angry resentful frown to Kat's brow.

'I don't want you to over-exert yourself.'

'How can you be so sure?' He seemed to be in the mood to discompose her some more as he leaned back against a mosaic dolphin on the tiled side of the pool. 'That you won't fall in love with a pretty face? Don't be so quick to pour scorn!' he warned, as an indignant denial trembled angrily on her tongue. 'You may be looking for a guy's inner strength but it's quite likely you'll see his tight behind first.'

Under the glittering mockery of his too blue eyes, heat flooded Kat's face. 'I don't look at men's bottoms, tight or otherwise.' She tried to compress her full and sexy lips into a prim and prissy line and failed in a way that delighted Matt.

'Except professionally, of course...' he added with mock solemnity.

Was this his way of telling her he'd seen straight through her *professional* gawping earlier? If it is, I don't want to know, she decided, gritting her teeth and rising above the malicious taunt.

'All right, let's say for the sake of argument that you're not a bottom girl. What happens if you meet a rat who just happens to fulfil all your girlhood dreams...?'

What, indeed?

'You'd know about that, I suppose?' If ever a man was the embodiment of female dreams, he was it!

'Why, Miss Wray, I do believe you're telling me I'm

pretty! I don't know what to say…' He performed a parody
of coy and modest that would have had her laughing if she
hadn't been so tense and suspicious.

'We can only live in hope.' This drew a deep wildly
attractive rumble of laughter from him. 'And actually I was
thinking of the rat part.'

'The point I'm trying to make—'

'In a long-winded way.'

'Is that when it comes to the crunch your lofty principles
might prove lacking.'

'If they do, you'll be the first to know,' she snapped
sarcastically. 'Are you ready to do a few more exercises
before we call it a day?'

'No, I'm ready for a swim.'

'I don't think you're ready.'

He listened with an expression of deep interest, then gave
her a wicked little grin and launched himself smoothly towards the deep end of the pool.

Kat had little choice but to follow him, even though she
wasn't the best swimmer in the world and, given the choice,
she didn't normally venture out of her depth. He had covered a good half of the pool in a lazy but efficient crawl
before she caught up with him. He was lying on his back,
squinting up through half-closed eyes at the elaborate mu-
rals of toga-clad women on the high ceiling.

'Hell, that felt good!'

Kat began to inexpertly tread water. 'That was a stupid
thing to do!'

'Your breathing could do with some work,' he observed,
regarding her red-cheeked breathlessness critically.

This was one piece of provocation too many for Kat,
who had been scared stiff that he'd get into trouble in deep
water and she'd be unable to help him.

'I didn't come here to be your lifeguard, or for that matter your nursemaid!' she yelled. 'If you're going to ignore
everything I say, I don't see much point in staying!' At that

moment she swallowed a large mouthful of water. Coughing and choking, her uncoordinated thrashing movements sent her head under the water. Panic kept her there longer than was necessary and a strong arm brought her back up.

When her head re-emerged above the water, Matt's arms were linked gently under her armpits.

'You're fine,' the voice beside her ear soothed persuasively—so persuasively, in fact, that if she hadn't felt as if she'd swallowed half the pool she might have believed him. 'Just relax.'

Easier said than done! Kat fought back the instinct that made her want to claw wildly at him.

'Good girl,' he approved as she allowed her head to rest against his shoulder. 'Let me do the work.'

Every professional instinct told Kat she should do nothing of the sort, but her fright had taken the fight clear out of her.

'You'll…'

'*Break?* I don't think so. Besides, the water is doing all the work; you're as light as a feather.'

'That's a novelty.'

Her passive acceptance of his aid lasted until she felt the bottom of the pool under her toes. The arm looped across her ribcage fell away as she struggled to regain her feet.

'You can't swim!'

The virulence of his biting accusation took her by surprise. 'Of course I can. I just can't swim as well as you.' She pushed back her drenched hair from her face with unsteady hands.

An image of his streamlined body moving through the water appeared in her head. He was as supple and confident as a seal in the water. Even in a panic-stricken state, part of her had registered his grace and casual elegance. She instinctively knew that under normal circumstances he would be just as rivetingly, breathtakingly elegant on dry land.

'You call that swimming?' His brows drew into a scornful dark line.

Kat glared mutinously back. Hadn't she been humiliated enough without him rubbing salt in the wound? Still he didn't let it go! It was *her* near-death experience, for heaven's sake!

'Why the hell swim out of your depth when you knew you couldn't handle it?'

Kat still felt out of her depth; she felt that way every time she looked at him. 'Well, someone had to be there to save you if you overreached yourself!' she yelled back, stomping abruptly towards the steps and sitting down in the shallow water with a bump. Her knees were feeling the after effects of her little adventure and her head was spinning. With a sigh she let her head fall weakly to her lap.

'She was going to save me…?' Matt repeated under his breath as he made his way towards her. Out of the water it was a slow, arduous process. '*She* was going to save *me*…! he repeated. A slow grin spread across his face as he shook his head wonderingly from side to side. 'Are you all right?'

Kat lifted her head. Her face was pale but otherwise she didn't look too bad… Actually, she looked deeply desirable. His body responded lustfully. If asked at that moment he would have fiercely denied that he'd ever thought her insipidly pretty.

'I'm fine.' Thankfully the nausea had receded.

'Are all our sessions going to be this dramatic?'

Kat shook her head. 'There aren't going to be any more. I really don't think this is going to work out.' She was just amazed that he couldn't see this too. 'You must see that.'

'Why must I?'

Kat's jaw tightened. 'We don't get on.'

'Do you only treat patients you like?'

Now she knew he was being deliberately obtuse. 'This

isn't dislike. This is a total clash of personalities! I'm not—'

'Throwing in the towel?' he suggested smoothly.

'I'm no quitter!' she insisted defiantly. 'I just can't work in this atmosphere.'

'Ah, the *atmosphere*...'

Kat didn't like the way he said that one bit at all. She shot him a worried furtive glance from under the sweep of her wet eyelashes.

'Be careful!' she said sharply as, with his left leg extended stiffly, he lowered himself smoothly down beside her.

Kat didn't know if the hair-roughened flesh of his thigh had come to rest against her own deliberately, but she did know that it was the last straw! The hot liquid sensation that pooled low in her belly was even more debilitating than the strange, light-headed, floaty feeling and the weakness that afflicted all her limbs simultaneously.

Matt watched as a fine tremor ran through her entire body. 'Are you cold?'

Cold, hot...? Both...neither. Kat didn't have the faintest idea, and cared even less.

'Perhaps we should leave...?'

'I've told you, I am leaving.' As soon as she could trust herself to stand up.

Matt allowed his exasperation to show. 'You need a job; I need a physio...' If he'd said what else he needed... needed *badly,* as it happened...he'd really spook her, and probably earn himself a lot of bad publicity into the bargain!

It occurred to him it was bit late in the day to remember office protocol... There were excuses... This wasn't an office... This was a hot steamy place where a guy didn't wear many clothes to hide his interest! Actually, it was a bit of a relief; after the paraplegic scare he'd been assured there would be no problems on that score. Only when the feeling had returned to his toes and his legs there had been no corresponding awakening in vital areas—not until now!

'How about if I promise to be a good boy and do everything you tell me…?'

A distressed moan escaped from Kat's throat as her fevered imagination came up with several things she'd like to tell him to do; the *things* could only be termed exercises in the loosest possible sense! Why did he have to be so vibrantly male? she wondered despairingly.

Her teeth came together so hard it hurt. '*I can't!*' she told him in a strangled voice.

'Of course you can.'

Kat lifted her head from her contemplation of her white-knuckled fingers with a snap; her eyes were blazing. 'I can't stay here,' she grated in a goaded voice. 'It might be different if I was a typist or something.' Typing didn't require a person to lay her hands on her boss's bare skin. There was nothing even vaguely clinical about the almost overwhelming urge she had to place her hands against his solid chest.

'I don't see the distinction.'

Kat's nostrils flared and her cheeks grew hot with shame. 'I can't…can't look at you the way I should look at a patient.'

There was a frustratingly blank look of incomprehension in Matt's eyes.

'It's not…*proper!*'

CHAPTER FIVE

YOU didn't have to have a razor-sharp intellect to figure out the opposite of proper was improper. Nobody had ever accused Matt of being a slouch in the brains department.

There was honesty and then there was simple-minded stupidity! A sane person didn't introduce stray bullets into a crowded place, and what she had just said was just as reckless and even more explosive! The way things were going, it hardly seemed worth taking her foot out of her mouth!

'*Oh, God!*' she groaned, lifting her hands to her face and closing her eyes tightly. 'I can't believe you made me say that.' She glared resentfully at him.

'Let me get this right...' he began cautiously. There was such a thing as a man hearing what he wanted to.

He sounded stunned—who wouldn't under the circumstances? The women he knew were probably shy, retiring types who probably waited a whole *twenty-four hours* before they announced they didn't trust themselves in the same room as him!

Why did I say it? she despaired, hugging her humiliation quite literally to herself as, elbows braced against her knees, she began to rock gently to and fro. It was only matter of time before that shock would turn to smug amusement...or, worse, *pity and embarrassment!*

'That didn't come out right at all.' Not at all and there wouldn't have been a problem!

'I don't think it left much room for misinterpretation.'

The rat looked as though he was enjoying her discomfiture.

'You are harbouring...what was the word...? Improper,

81

yes, *improper* thoughts about me? I thought you said that you didn't even like me...and you *definitely* didn't fancy me...' he taunted in the manner of a sleek, well-fed feline tormenting a mesmerised mouse.

'There's no need to make a song and dance about it. I know what I said,' she snarled belligerently. 'And I still don't *like* you,' she brooded, serving up a very unsmitten glare for his benefit.

'So this is sex, pure and simple?'

Even if your pride was in tatters, in her book it was still worth clinging to. Kat's hands fell away from her flaming face. Her chin came up. She might be in corner but it wasn't in her nature to submit without a fight.

'Hearing you use terms like *pure* is fairly ironic,' she observed scornfully. Anything less pure than the self-satisfied glint in his eyes would be hard to imagine.

I could have just packed my bags and walked away...she brooded wistfully. I could have kept my mouth shut and my dignity intact. But no, that would have been too easy! I had to go and announce it.

'It's not the end of the world... Sexual awareness between men and women is perfectly normal, and if it makes you feel any better it wasn't exactly news to me.'

Kat groaned. 'Well, it wouldn't be, would it? You think you're irresistible.'

'It seems you share my opinion.'

She opened her mouth and nothing emerged but a little choking sound.

'It makes a man feel good to know he hasn't lost his touch.'

Kat cast a look of loathing over his oh, so perfect features. Was she meant to believe he'd even know what self-doubt was if it hit him over the head?

A tiny smile of relief flickered across her face as her madly racing brain came up with the perfect get-out story— well, not *perfect,* but she was in no position to be picky.

'Do you *honestly* think I'd be stupid enough to say so if I actually was misguided enough to find you attractive?'

Her tinkling laughter made it sound as though it was the best joke she'd heard in ages—it was a bonus that he didn't look as though he enjoyed the sound.

'Let me be frank.'

'Is there any way of stopping you?' he wondered drily.

'The bottom line is, deep down, you still think Drusilla had ulterior motives when she gave me this job.'

'Don't you?'

Kat bit her lip. 'It does seem possible,' she conceded.

'And this is relevant because...?' She looked so strung out, he almost let her off the hook.

'I was getting to that,' she snapped, directing a look of dislike at his handsome features. 'When I said...' Kat found she couldn't bring herself to repeat what she'd said. 'My job, by its nature, is very...*tactile*,' she babbled. 'I simply meant that I can't work properly if every time I look at you I'm wondering if you think I've got a private agenda.'

'You mean you're worried I'll think you've decided to overlook major flaws like my millions?'

Her eyes narrowed. 'Don't forget your arrogance.'

'In short, you're concerned I'll think you're enjoying your job too much?'

'If so far is anything to go by, there's not much chance of that...' Love wasn't turning out to be at all what she'd expected. 'But that's exactly what I mean!' she exclaimed, not particularly bothered by the contradictory nature of her statement. 'I'm going to spend all my time worrying you'll think I'm making a pass at you, and going by your reaction just now I'm obviously right!' Kat's shoulders slumped in relief... It had actually sounded plausible!

Matt could have driven several trucks through the holes in her rambling explanation, but he didn't have the heart to mention it.

'Pity...'

Now, don't go reading anything into that, Kat remonstrated herself firmly. He's just got *that* sort of voice and *those* sort of eyes. Sizzle and smoulder were the norm for Matt Devlin.

'I thought it evened things out... No, you're not running out now!' he announced firmly as she began to surge purposefully to her feet. A strong hand stopped her mid-surge.

He might have been having a problem with his leg, but the fingers clamped around her upper arm made it pretty clear the weakness didn't extend to his upper limbs; she couldn't have budged if she'd wanted to, and since he'd touched her things had got a bit ambivalent on the escape front. She subsided weakly.

'Would it make things less...*improper*—' God, but he loved the sound of that word '—if I sack you?'

Was he trying to be funny? 'I've just told you, *improper* has nothing to do with it; and you can't sack me, I've already resigned.' She sighed and tried to act as if the touch of his hand on her arm wasn't making her ridiculously susceptible body get all hot and *very* bothered!

'The way I see it, the problem is you don't look at me and think patient...?'

'I've told you!' Kat was very conscious of her aching breasts as they chafed against the restrictions of the imprisoning Lycra.

'I know, I know, I got it all wrong...' Impatiently he brushed aside her heated response.

'Don't humour me,' she gritted. 'I'm serious.' If she said it often enough, she might start believing it herself.

'Do you think I look at you and think clinical practitioner?' he asked abruptly.

Kat felt pretty certain he was working up to a major insult. 'I'm not sure I want to know what sort of things your head is cluttered with,' she replied, sounding seriously priggish.

'Shall we leave the sordid state of my subconscious out

of this?' It sounded like an afterthought when he added, 'Are you trying to tell me that your thoughts are as pure as the driven snow?'

'Of course I'm not,' she responded crossly. Heaven help her if he asked her what she did mean, because she didn't have the faintest idea.

'For the sake of argument, let's take the worst case scenario—you are consumed by lust every time you look at me.'

Kat could hear the strained note of uneasiness in her scornful laughter; she just hoped he couldn't too.

'Why are you getting so het up about this? You're not my doctor; you're not misusing a position of power. Look at me!' he instructed her, cupping her chin so she didn't have much option. 'Do I look like someone who's going to be sexually abused unless he wants to be?'

Did that mean he wanted to be? Kat's eyes flickered wildly around the room but there was no way she could avoid his eyes for more than a few seconds; only she knew that once she'd made eye contact with those startling blue eyes she'd only be able to escape when he decided she could. It was bizarre, but she was acting like the sort of weak helpless female she detested. She had never encountered a man who made her feel impotent and out of control. Was this what being in love was about? If so, God knew how it had ever caught on!

'We're not talking medical malpractice here, Kathleen,' he continued in a softer, more persuasive tone. He could be more persuasive without exerting himself than any man had a right to be! 'We're not talking sordid, unnatural practices...' One dark, strongly delineated brow rose to a satirical slant. 'At least, I'm not.' He waited politely for Kat to recover from her choking fit before continuing, 'We're talking about nothing more sinister than bit of good old-fashioned chemistry.'

'This sort of talk is…is…inappropriate.' She carefully avoided all mention of wildly exciting.

She had a deliciously quaint turn of phrase.

Her hand came up to remove his from her face; she was going to be firm and calm about this. While she was being firm and calm, her fingers mysteriously became inextricably tangled with his… The chain of thought led to her picturing other parts of them tangled in more intimate ways. She gave a little gasp, shocked rigid by her own depravity.

'Why don't you let me decide what's appropriate?'

Right at the moment, he seemed to think it was appropriate to draw her hand onto his lap. His face filled her vision as he maintained an apparently effortless grip on her eyes. She felt him separate each digit individually as he spread her fingers out against the hard warm flesh of his thigh.

The hunger curled low in her belly became urgent; she exhaled in a series of short, sharp breaths.

'I thought you wanted to get rid of me,' she mumbled.

'That was before.'

Before I made myself out to be an easy sexual target…? It was a humiliating but pretty obvious conclusion to draw.

'Aren't you afraid this isn't all part of my master plan to get you up the aisle?'

He dismissed her spiky words with a tolerant, almost caressing smile. 'I don't think this situation is the sort of thing you can plan for. I think that's what's bothering you most.'

Kat could have told him how completely wrong he was about that, only the telling would have involved explaining that at that precise moment the male scent of his skin was the single most bothersome factor in her life. It was probably a bit late in the day to be wise and cautious, but she kept her mouth shut anyhow.

'When I said before, it evens things up…'

'D…Did you?' she stammered.

'Did you understand what I meant?'

Kat didn't understand anything! She shook her head and felt her wet hair slither down her back; the sodden weight of it felt cold against her overheated skin. 'This isn't supposed to be happening.'

She watched in a bemused fashion as a smile that managed to combine ferocity with tenderness slowly curved his deliciously sensuous lips.

'This sort of thing happens all the time, Blondie.'

Kat gulped. Compared to this, drowning had been a bit of light relief! She was so far gone it didn't even occur to pick him up on the 'Blondie'!

'Not to me it doesn't.' She had responded without thinking...so what was new?

Matt picked up a hank of darkened blonde hair and rubbed the silky wet texture between his thumb and forefinger before brushing the tip teasingly against the tip of her chin.

'You feel embarrassed...'

Kat could hear a definite hint of hysteria in her bitter laugh. 'You could say that,' she croaked hoarsely. 'And so will you,' she predicted, 'if you think I want you to do this.'

He had an infuriating habit of ignoring anything he didn't want to hear.

'Embarrassed because you told me you felt aroused. Men don't always have the luxury of disguising the fact they are aroused.' He watched her lusciously fringed eyes widen as the implication of what he said dawned on her. 'Especially when they're dressed the way I am,' he elaborated with a complete lack of self-consciousness. 'That's what I meant when I said it evens things up. I'm not lying to spare your feelings,' he promised. 'You can check if you like.'

A soft whimper emerged from her dry throat. The thought of what checking would involve had sent her heart-rate into overdrive! The eerie, echoing pounding against her eardrums of her own hormones rushing around her body was almost deafening. And, to make matters worse, her eyes, which up to this point had been firmly glued to his face, now showed a lamentable tendency to wander. If she allowed them to plot their own route Kat didn't need to be psychic to figure out where they'd end up!

A few seconds before, she'd have sworn it wasn't possible to be more conscious of where her fingers lay. She had been wrong—big-time! She froze; the only safe thing to do was not move at all. That way there was no chance anything she did could be misconstrued.

'Pretty nurses…bed baths…every young and not so young man's nightmare, I would think.'

'It hasn't been mine…until now, if you know what I mean.'

She wasn't in the mood for twenty questions. 'I don't,' she said shortly as she nervously dabbed the beads of moisture form her upper lip with the tip of her tongue. The gesture drew his hot hungry gaze like honey drew a bee.

'Let's just say I didn't have a hard time keeping my libido in check.'

Kat's mouth opened in soundless O of wonder.

'Are you saying you *couldn't*…?'

Hadn't felt like, would have been more accurate; however, now he could see what an improvement this slant could put on things.

'There's a very fine line dividing apathy and inability…' So far, true and accurate. 'But a man starts to wonder,' he admitted, with the air of someone making a painful confession.

It wasn't an outright lie. A more imaginative man might have lain awake wondering; it just so happened that he'd had more urgent things to worry about at the time, such as learning to walk again and keeping his company safe from the circling sharks!

Kat laughed nervously. She couldn't decide if he was serious.

So he was stretching a point; Matt's conscience was flexible enough to cope. It had succeeded in taking her mind off packing her bags, and Matt had every intention of putting all his not inconsiderable powers of persuasion into preventing her from doing that. He'd worry later about why it was so damned important all of a sudden.

'When I first came to, I couldn't feel anything from the waist down...' This time he didn't have to fake the dull note of repressed horror in his voice.

Kat felt his fingers tighten against the delicate bones of her collarbone. It hurt, but not as much as the surge of empathy that swelled her tender heart to breaking point.

'But that was only temporary...'

'Sure, my spinal cord turned out to be intact.' He shrugged and the thick lashes momentarily cut off the glow of those articulate eyes of his. 'But a man tends to wonder in that sort of situation...'

If the dark, brooding expression in his eyes was any indicator, Kat didn't think that any of his thoughts had been pleasant.

'I had a lot of time on my hands to think about all the things I took for granted and whether I had got the guts to go on as half a man.'

'Of course you would!' Her protest was instinctive; her conviction went bone-deep.

The words emerged more forcibly than she'd have liked, but she had no problem with the content. The idea of Matt Devlin giving up on anything, let alone life, struck her as just too ridiculous to contemplate. She might not have known him for long, but from what she'd seen so far he had the sort of iron will that would conquer any obstacle.

'I'm glad I was never put to the test, but thanks for the vote of confidence.'

Without thinking, Kat raised her hand to emphasise the point she wanted to make.

'There's more to man than a...' It was at the precise moment her hand brushed against the object she'd been dismissing as unimportant.

Matt watched the disintegration of her composure with a fascinated eye. It was hard to follow the precise sequence of events, things went so fast, but as far as he could tell she pressed the offending hand to her mouth at about the same moment the colour fled her face. Micro-seconds later, her eyes were drawn irresistibly to the cause of her discomfort. He could almost feel the heat from the wave of rosy colour that rose from her neck and took only a handful of seconds to cover every inch of visible skin.

Matt was so engrossed by the response that she'd already babbled *sorry* half a dozen times before he roused himself enough to silence her. The simplest way to do it—and he wasn't man who liked to complicate matters—seemed to be to kiss her.

The touch of his lips against her ear was so delicate Kat couldn't be sure whether it was the mere suggestion of a kiss that sent a shiver up her spine or the real thing.

'I should be thanking you for dispelling the spectre of impotence,' he whispered huskily.

There was no confusion about the next kiss—it was the real thing and then some! Kat had been kissed lots of times before; some had been more pleasant than others, but none had been like this!

This kiss was several light years removed from *pleasant!* It began unalarmingly enough; the light, almost soothing sensation of his lips against hers only lasted a few heart-stopping seconds. It was time enough for all the tension to magically drain from her body, time enough for her to ache with longing. By the time he plunged headlong into the welcome offered by her tremulous parted lips, restraint was a dim and distant memory.

She responded to everything his lips demanded of her, and the scariest thing was the slow-motion action replay later revealed to a dismayed Kat that she would have given more if that was what he'd wanted… She would have given everything!

Kat's eyes stayed closed for a long time afterwards. Matt could see the delicate tracery of blue veins that showed through the thin, almost transparent delicacy of gently fluttering lids.

'*Oh, my God!*' she groaned huskily when her eyes did open.

Her slightly unfocused gaze slid immediately to his mouth. The amazement tinged with appreciative awe in that look was deeply flattering to a bloke's ego. The ache in Matt's loins kicked another jaw-clenching notch.

Kat became visibly flustered to discover her hands were still linked firmly around his neck. With a dismayed squeak, she pulled them away and proceeded to wedge them under her firm thighs. His own fingers itched to follow their example. Maybe she didn't trust them not to wander… Now, that was a *very* agreeable thought.

'It's been a while.' Maybe absence had made him appreciate the simple pleasures of kissing, either that or it had been an exceptionally great kiss. 'I thought maybe I'd forgotten how.'

As if! Kat lifted a hand to her spinning head.

'You haven't!' she breathed, too distracted to think about what he might read into her words.

His head fell back and, eyes half-closed, he exhaled noisily. The action caused all sorts of fascinating things to happen to the powerful muscles of his chest and shoulders. Kat could have named each muscle and tendon involved; it wasn't as if she was learning anything new, so why was she totally mesmerised by the spectacle?

'One hell of a chemical reaction.' Supporting his leg between his hands, he eased his position, and she saw the tight muscles of his belly clench in anticipation of the jarring movement.

'One hell of a kisser!' she indicted grimly.

Matt didn't make the error of mistaking this for a compliment.

'I can't think why you did anything so stupid!' she continued in the same fretful tone as she struggled, with limited success, to throw off the strange heavy lethargy which made it hard to think straight.

'Why do you think I did it...?' His glance moved with crude significance over her lush curves.

Kat gave a gasp; she was too angry to guard her tongue as she hit back.

'Like a kid who's just got his favourite toy back, you couldn't resist trying it out?'

After a startled pause, Matt began to laugh; the sound was so warm and uninhibited and so deeply infectious that she found it hard not to respond with a grin of her own. But as abruptly as he had begun laughing he stopped, and his expression became hard and almost calculating.

'Maybe I thought I had nothing to lose...?' he suggested. Kat got the feeling his infuriatingly off-hand shrug was meant to annoy her. 'I mean, what was the worst you could do? You're already wimping out on the job...' he reminded her scornfully. The blue eyes were uncomfortably intent when they came to rest on her flushed face. 'You *are* wimping out?'

'I'm leaving,' she corrected with dignity.

He sighed. 'Drusilla's going to very disappointed.'

Kat gave a snort of disbelief. 'Like you care! I was under the impression you went out of your way to disoblige your mother. I suppose you're relieved to know you're in full working order?' she added carelessly.

Another laugh was wrenched from deep in his chest. 'You have quite a way with words, Kathleen...'

'Kat.' The correction was automatic.

'I prefer Kathleen. I can't say the subject has been keeping me awake nights.'

'I thought as much.'

'But, yes, it's not unwelcome news.'

'All part of the recovery process.' It was a bit late to wheel out the objectivity.

'I thought you were going to say it was all part of the service.'

Kat winced. Considering her wanton behaviour, this was a perfectly legitimate thing to think.

'Dream on!' To her critical ears the retort smacked uncomfortably of adolescent badinage.

'I've nothing against dreamers, but I've always thought of myself as more the dynamic action type myself,' he explained with a mock-heroic pose that poked fun at the image the media liked to lumber him with.

At any other time, his antics might have made her laugh; right now, his boast inspired fear. If he got active on the kissing front again, she'd be a goner!

'Are you trying to shock me?' She put on her best heard-it-all, seen-it-all-before expression.

His grin was unapologetic. 'I think I already have. But then that's only fair because you don't always say or do what I'm expecting, either.' There was a flare of wry amusement in his blue eyes as he looked into her angry and discomposed face. 'That puts you in a fairly unique category.'

'Like a freak?'

'Would I be that unkind?' Her expression spoke volumes; he grinned. 'More an enigma, a lovely contradiction. If I promise not to kiss you again will you reconsider?'

'Why should I believe you?'

'I get the feeling playing the integrity card won't work with you...'

Kat fixed a scornful glare on her face. She could hardly remind him that it was her own trustworthiness she was concerned about, not his! She watched with some anxiety as he got slowly to his feet. It was incredibly hard staying where she was when every impulse was telling her to get up and help him. He reached for his cane and it slid to the floor.

Kat leaned across and grabbed it; she held it out to him. 'Be careful,' she pleaded.

Matt took the ebony handle. 'You've resigned, remember?'

Her eyes remained on his slim strong fingers curled around the handle. 'Old habits die hard,' she admitted, releasing the cane.

'You need the job, don't you?' he stated flatly as she too got up from the floor. 'And by all accounts you do it well.'

Kat sighed and avoided his eyes. If she stayed she'd be able to wipe the slate clean of her mum's debts in one fell swoop. She was tempted—there was no use pretending otherwise. The big question was, could she do it and not become another notch in his bedpost?

'All I've done so far is nearly drown myself.' It wasn't a record that screamed competence.

Matt watched as she dropped her head forward, ran her fingers roughly through her heavy mane of pale, water-darkened hair, then straightened up and with a flicking motion sent it all swishing damply backwards off her face. He could tell that she had put no more thought into the action than she would washing her hands.

Matt, who had been seduced—sometimes successfully—by experts, found it the single most seductive thing he'd ever seen. Then again, he reflected with a self derisive smile, the way things were heading maybe he'd think the same thing if he saw her washing her hands! Whatever his mother's intentions had been—and actually he didn't much care—she'd really put the cat among the pigeons this time!

'Drusilla's going to want to know why you decided to throw her generosity back in her face.'

Kat felt a twinge of guilt. 'I'm no longer sure that Drusilla was being all that generous,' she grumbled.

'If you're worried I'll want to make up for lost time on the lust front, I could provide myself with some female companionship.' He watched to see if her reaction to this suggestion was all that he'd hoped—it was. 'Would that make you feel more comfortable?'

Kat could hardly believe what she was hearing.

'It's as simple as that, is it?' She gazed at this classic example of arrogant manhood in undisguised amazement. At the back of her mind lurked the uncomfortable fact that knowing Matt was sleeping with some willing lovely would make her nights agony.

'I have a wide circle of friends…many of whom are female.'

'Who would drop everything, including their knickers, if you whistle?' She looked him up and down with a contemptuous smile, then her defiant expression slowly faded, leaving a shade of fear in its place. You bet they would! He really was in a class of his own, the sort of man women didn't say no to! It was mortifying to realise she had to class herself amongst their number.

Matt's eyes sparkled with barely subdued laughter.

'That's a very coarse thing for a *nice* girl to say,' he announced gravely.

Despite his tone Kat didn't think he looked particularly offended by her vulgarity; she, on the other hand, was horrified by her display of cattiness.

He might just as well have said I'm boring; I bet none of those girls in his little—pardon, *big*—black book are nice.

'Who said I'm *nice?*' she snapped belligerently.

'I expect my mother will when she eventually rings.'

Kat picked up her tee-shirt from where she'd dropped it. 'Some days in the hospital I would see dozens of patients. It never occurred to me that looking after one patient…'

'Client.'

She received the correction in much the spirit it had been offered and ground her teeth.

'It didn't occur to me that one individual *client* could be more labour-intensive than all of them put together!' In her ignorance, she'd actually thought it would be a luxury not to have to worry about the next appointment. She had been looking forward to the prospect of giving her one patient the benefit of her undivided attention... She hadn't reckoned on it being *this* undivided, though!

'So you turned up here thinking you were on to a cushy number and I came here thinking I was going to get some peace and quiet. We were both wrong.'

'I'm not afraid of hard work!' she countered, bristling furiously at the implication she was work-shy.

'Great!' he cut back swiftly. 'Stay, because I have it on good authority that I'm *very* hard work.'

'Do you ever give up?' she wondered wearily.

'Not when I want something, and I want you...to rehabilitate me.'

Kat was uncomfortably aware of the dew of sweat that had broken out over her entire body. She had no doubt whatever that the pause had been deliberate and, like a fool, she obliged him by falling for the bait.

She cleared her dry throat. 'I think that's beyond my capabilities,' she told him hoarsely. 'I think your best bet is Drusilla coming up with a wife who can keep you in line.'

'Are you applying for the job?'

Was he doing a little carrot-dangling, or did he just enjoy seeing her squirm?

Although she'd been displaying the intellectual capacity of a donkey just lately, the particular carrot he was mockingly dangling held no appeal. Matt Devlin might be the most attractive man she'd ever met, she might be filled with lustful cravings every time she thought about him, she might have fallen for him big-time—but she couldn't think of many more alarming fates for a girl than to be married to him. For starters, he wouldn't be faithful. Hadn't he already made his opinion of fidelity quite clear? She resolutely ignored the tiny voice of dissent in some distant corner of her mind that inconveniently pointed out it might also be a wildly exciting fate.

'I've no objection to being kept in line by the right woman,' he announced. 'Only I'd prefer to pick my own.' He stood there oozing male virility, looking so much like the embodiment of all her dreams that she felt like weeping.

She coaxed her lips into a superior smile. 'Men always think it was *their* idea,' she sniffed.

'You terrify me!'

Not half as much as you do me. 'Don't give up hope. I'm sure there's a poor deluded soul somewhere out there for you.' She made the possibility sound extremely remote.

Her venom didn't seem to bother him. 'So you think we all have a soul mate out there?'

His question took her aback. 'Most people I know seem to think they have several,' she responded, hiding her discomfort behind a caustic tongue. When she actually reviewed the alarming proportion of her married friends who had already split up, she came to the conclusion her cynicism was actually pretty well founded. 'I suppose they're working on the theory that if they try often enough they might eventually strike it lucky.'

'Do I detect a note of cynicism…?'

'What did you expect, a hopeless romantic?' she challenged. 'If you want one of those I know several…'

All of whom would take one look at him and… Of course! Why didn't I think of that earlier? she wondered as she was hit by a neat solution to her present dilemma. And perhaps I can call it progress that I'm willing to admit I have a problem.

She made an attempt to look at her problem—all six feet four of him—objectively, and felt a stab of sexual awareness so strong she couldn't breathe for several seconds.

She gathered her wits ruthlessly and gave herself a sharp

mental shake. Desperate measures were definitely called for! He was right about one thing. She did need this job. It was being the latest in long line of sexual conquests she didn't need. If he hadn't been temporarily unattached and making up for lost time he wouldn't look twice at her, she decided, wrinkling her nose as she concentrated on the details of her plan.

If she introduced Matt to the sort of girl who actually liked her men arrogant, opinionated and conceited, he wouldn't have the time or inclination to taunt her and she could do her job, get paid and get out!

'I'll stay…on conditions…'

'I've told you, Blondie…'

'No *Blondies!*' she bellowed, planting her hands on her hips and glaring up at him.

Her stance drew attention to the slenderness of her waist and the undulating nature of the rest of her figure. Matt repressed a sigh… *Pure poetry,* whether static or in motion.

'A mere slip of the tongue, Kathleen,' he soothed. 'When I said no kissing, I meant it…' His mock meekness vanished as he continued, 'Unless, of course, you kiss me first. Then a bloke would be obliged to respond, don't you think…?' There was a wolfish gleam in his eyes as he adopted an innocent tone to appeal to her judgement.

Two darker spots stood out amidst the delicate wild rose tint of her smooth cheeks. So he was relying on her lack of willpower. And the awful part was his confidence might not be unjustified. The sooner she got him together with Emma, the better!

If Emma's ex-husband had been *half* as bad as she made out then Emma definitely liked her men mean, nasty and with an over-inflated idea of their own importance. If it wasn't for the fact that at their last meeting Emma had announced to a slightly shocked Kat that it was her firm intention to lose no time making up for the fact her ex-husband had up to that point been her only lover, Kat wouldn't have dreamt of throwing them together.

'I've got a friend who is a better swimmer than me.' And then some. No male with red blood could watch Emma dive into a pool and not be wildly impressed by her athletic prowess, not to mention her supple streamlined body, Kat decided miserably.

'That's no great recommendation.'

'She's dived...dove...whatever—' she finished up in a grammatical tangle '—competitively at international level.'

Matt's sable brows shot up at her enthusiasm to sell the other woman. 'Actually, all we need is someone who can stay afloat. At a pinch, you'll do, so long as we stay in the shallows.'

'No!' Kat exclaimed, unable to disguise her panic. There was no way she was going to strip down to what amounted to her undies in the same room as Matt ever again. There was such a thing as asking for trouble! 'If I told her what to do would you be willing for her to supervise your activities in here?'

'What makes you think this friend of yours will automatically want to take me on?'

Kat allowed her eyes to dwell for a painful moment on the damp skin of Matt's sleek powerful torso before she raised them to his strikingly handsome face.

'Oh, she'll take you on, all right,' she said dully.

'I didn't think you were *that* freaked out,' he murmured, a furrow of concern appearing in his brow. 'I'm not sure avoiding the issue is going to solve anything. You really ought to face your fears.'

Not likely! she thought, developing a sudden and intense interest in her toes. Some fears were best avoided altogether!

'Those are my terms—take it or leave it.'

His magnificent shoulders lifted; he gave her a languid smile. 'You're the boss.'

Kat discovered she was intensely suspicious of his easy capitulation. Maybe paranoia was catching, she mused. 'And don't you forget it,' she replied gruffly.

CHAPTER SIX

'HE'S got a great body!' Emma reflected with a predatory little purr.

Kat, who had been coping remarkably well up to this point with the success of her plan, felt her fixed smile slip.

She knew his body, not Emma. She knew it, if not intimately, then better than most casual acquaintances. When she worked on his injured soft tissue and freshly knitted bones, she managed to retain a satisfactory degree of objectivity. The same couldn't be said for the occasions when their hands accidentally brushed, or her knee made contact with his. She had obsessed for hours after over the illicit thrill of such incidents.

Kat's conscience was giving her trouble. It would be a pretty calculating, selfish act if I took advantage of a friend's fragile emotional state and pushed her into Matt's arms just because I can't trust myself! I must have been off my head to even think about it! Kat's tense shoulders relaxed; she felt a whole lot better having ditched the crazy idea.

'Tell me straight, would I be treading on your toes if I—'

Startled, Kat looked over at her friend and saw a defiant grin appear on Emma's face.

'—get close and personal...?' she asked in an abrupt way.

It would seem pushing wouldn't be needed!

Kat swallowed past the aching constriction in her throat. 'Would it matter if you were?' It was a bit late to remember how ruthlessly focused Emma could be when she wanted something.

'You don't pinch your best friend's feller…it's a definite no-no.'

This was a nightmare, and the irony was she had nobody but herself to blame for it. 'Well, he's not my feller.' Her smile carefully consigned the notion to comic fiction. 'I've only known him forty-eight hours. Hardly long enough to build up a deep and meaningful relationship.'

'What's time got to do with it?'

What, indeed? Kat found herself resenting Emma's simplistic outlook on life. She took a deep breath and smiled.

'Go for it!' she advised briskly. 'As long as you remember he's recuperating.'

'I'll be very gentle,' Emma promised with a cat's-got-the-cream look on her face. 'I've got to go,' she said, glancing at her watch. 'I'll see you soon.' She blew a kiss in Kat's direction.

'Wait!' Kat cried, scrambling to her feet hurriedly. She barely noticed the sundry items she'd knocked off the dressing table in her haste.

'What?' Emma, hand on the doorhandle, stood looking at her expectantly.

'Do you really think it's a good idea to do anything drastic so soon?' She saw Emma's elegant eyebrows lift and rushed on awkwardly. 'I'm not saying you shouldn't, but you don't actually really *know* Matt…'

Emma gave a little gasp; her dark eyes widened dramatically. 'Oh, my, I'm being dense here, aren't I? You can't stand the idea of anyone else touching him, can you?'

'No! Definitely not. No way… Of course not…!' In her anxiety to deny this claim the words came tumbling out in an incoherent jumble from Kat's mouth.

Emma looked at her friend's pink face sympathetically. She smiled that mysterious sphinx-like smile which even now, Kat decided miserably, Matt was probably fantasising about.

'I don't care who he touches.'

Emma patted her shoulder and gave her a quick hug. 'Sure you don't,' she agreed equably. 'I know this might sound strange coming from me, after I've been coming on like a right little...' She gave a tiny self-conscious grimace. 'But, you see, I know what it's like to love someone so much you'd do—' She broke off and took a deep breath. 'Just be careful.'

'Oh, I'm not going to do anything...'

'Whatever,' Emma agreed immediately, 'I take it I'm not required for pool duty any more?'

What could she say? Utterly mortified, Kat watched the door close. If Emma had guessed, how long would it be before...? With a loud wail she threw herself on the bed.

Kat had taken care dressing that evening. Her make-up was soft and subtle; it made her eyes look luminous and her lips inviting. Her hair was caught high on her head in a loose simple twist; the few silky tendrils that lay against her neck and face softened the overall look. The dress was nothing special, she didn't want him to think she was trying to compete...with anyone.

For all the reaction she'd had from Matt when she had nervously walked into the room, she might just as well have stayed in her joggers. She, on the other hand, had been reduced to a gibbering wreck the moment she'd seen him. He wore a dark shirt open at the neck and a pair of well-cut, loosely tailored pants.

'I'd much prefer to eat in my own room.' Actually, she'd have sooner not eaten at all; her stomach was churning.

The panelled dining room was a charming room, but Kat was in no mood to appreciate her surroundings or the beautifully presented food. She was insanely, stupidly, *fatally* aware of how attractive the man opposite her was, to such an extent she could barely string two words together. Face facts, girl, she told herself. The man only has to look at you and you're mush! It was pathetic, it was inexplicable, and it was a situation fraught with danger.

Matt watched her push the food around her plate. 'I didn't take you for a woman who picked at her food.'

Under normal circumstances he'd be right; under normal circumstances the comment wouldn't have made her bristle angrily. These weren't normal circumstances.

Kat dug her fork in a plump prawn and glared at it. She wasn't seeing the shellfish but Emma, and her sleek slender figure. She slowly lifted grey, unfriendly eyes to his.

'If you want to tell me I'm fat,' she said with a little toss of her blonde head, 'just go ahead, get it off your chest...I'm not touchy.'

Matt let out a long whistling breath from between clenched teeth. 'I can tell.'

'I'm quite happy with my body.'

Who wouldn't be? Matt included himself in that observation. 'I'm happy for you.'

'I've absolutely no intention of starving myself to a size ten.'

'I'm glad to hear it.' He was getting the impression that she harboured suspicions he was a man who thought anything above an eight was gross.

Kat, suspecting he was laughing at her, searched his face suspiciously. He returned the look gravely.

'Everything comes back into fashion eventually, so they say; I'm sure the same is true of the fuller figure.' He pushed back in his chair, carefully crossed one leg over the other, and waited for the explosion.

He saw her open her mouth to verbally flay him and then close it again when she caught onto the fact he was winding her up.

When he grinned like that, Kat had a hard time remembering she wasn't into shallow and meaningless relationships. Giving herself a sharp lecture on moral values, she hastily wiped the beginnings of a silly grin off her face.

'So maybe I am touchy,' she conceded grudgingly.
'Which is another reason for me to eat in my room.' She
eagerly seized the excuse.

'What, and add to the overworked staff's workload. I'm
shocked by your lack of consideration,' he remonstrated.

Kat lifted her eyes from her plate and discovered a mocking glint mingled with the exasperation in his riveting blue
eyes.

'I didn't mean that!' she snapped.

'I know what you meant.'

'You do?' Her body tensed.

'You'd prefer to be anywhere but in the same room as
me.'

'I know you think the world revolves around you, but...'
The sarcastic denial withered on her tongue as she encountered the wry expression on his face. So maybe he wasn't
as bad as all that. 'It's nothing personal,' she flung at him
in an exasperated tone.

'So you keep saying.'

'I just don't feel that sociable, and I'm used to going
home at the end of a bad day...' Her jerky gesture took in
the elaborate candlelit dinner table.

He could have pointed out that she'd been sociable
enough last night, when Joe had been a guest, and she
hadn't seemed actively seeking solitude when he'd discovered her that afternoon sitting relaxed and happy, her face
alight with animation as she'd chatted with the extra help
in the garden. Hell, he'd even heard her *giggle!* Predictably,
she'd pokered up when she'd seen him.

It wasn't as if he was jealous of a barely post-pubescent
teenager...that was unthinkable. The truth was, waiting for
her to make the first move was driving him slowly crazy.
What if she didn't...?

Matt had been turned down before—fewer times than
was good for his humility, possibly, but he'd always accepted the fact with a philosophical shrug. He didn't feel

even vaguely philosophical when he thought of Kathleen remaining unattainable. And why is she unattainable? Me and my big mouth is why. God, if this doesn't cure me of making grand gestures...

There was always the option of breaking his promise and making the first move. Yesterday he might have proudly sneered at the idea, only that had been a whole twenty-four hours ago. Today he'd experienced another long day and night—*especially night*—of wanting Kathleen so badly he could barely function. What was so great about pride, anyhow?

He looked up from his brooding contemplation of the bottom of his wine glass and discovered she was looking at him. God knew how long he'd been sitting there silently.

'So it's been a bad day...?'

'Not *bad* exactly...'

'But not good.' For a moment the downward droop of his heavy eyelids concealed his expression from her. 'Didn't it cheer you up seeing your friend Emma?'

Not as much as it did you, she thought swallowing past the painful stricture in her throat. 'It was nice to see her,' she replied with cool constraint. 'Did you find the session beneficial?'

'Extremely illuminating,' came the silky, ambiguous reply.

Before Kat could wonder what this enigmatic statement meant, he had changed the subject.

'And where is home?'

What he actually wanted to ask but wouldn't let himself was, *who* is at home? Despite her untouched air, Matt couldn't believe there wasn't some man waiting for a woman that looked like her... Why else would she be so anxious not to acknowledge the attraction between them?

Kat started; she hadn't been expecting the question. She raised a trembling hand to the spot at the base of her slender throat where a pulse throbbed wildly against the pale skin.

'You seem a little tense,' he mused lightly.

Like I needed reminding!

'I'm perfectly relaxed, thank you,' she assured him coldly.

Was it any wonder she was strung out tighter than a tennis racket? Forget relaxing chats over wine and good food, this conversation was fast becoming an interrogation. Lacking the opportunity to come up with a credible lie, she blurted out the truth.

'Just now, I suppose I'd have to say my suitcase is my home.'

She saw the tell-tale softening of his eyes and her chin went up angrily.

Great! Now not only does he think I'm a sexually repressed tease, he thinks I'm homeless, too...which I suppose, strictly speaking, I am.

'I like it that way,' she added fiercely. 'It's great being a free agent. I can do what I please; there's nothing to hold me down.'

It didn't sound particularly convincing, even to her. Kat hoped her remote expression would be discouraging enough to repress any inclinations Matt had to nose about some more into her personal affairs; which, when looked at objectively, were pretty much a mess.

'And nobody?'

'I've got plenty of friends.'

'Like the lovely Emma.' Smoothly, he reintroduced the brunette into the conversation.

Was it her imagination of was there a slight edge to his voice?

'Like Emma,' she agreed dully. Constantly dropping someone's name into the conversation was a sure sign of interest, according to the article she'd read in the dentist's waiting room the previous month.

'So you like to slob out at the end of the day...?'

'Relax,' she corrected pedantically.

'Me too. You should have said. We could have had supper picnic-style in front of the telly.'

Kat couldn't shake the impossibly foolish image in her head of them picnicking on a rug in front of a roaring log fire—her fantasy had undergone a slight seasonal adjustment—Matt was feeding her a tasty titbit and he was laughing tenderly. She wasn't the sort of girl who indulged in that sort of sickly, soft focus romanticism! Panic-stricken by the strength of the dream image's appeal, she fought her way back to reality.

'I couldn't possibly relax with you,' she protested hoarsely.

Matt looked more thoughtful than gutted by her unthinking response.

'Never say never, Kathleen. Actually, I don't think you're being totally honest with me, are you?' Maybe not with herself, either. 'What's the real reason you don't want to eat with me?'

Kat's clenched hands screwed up the edge of the white antique linen tablecloth into a tight ball. She supposed if push came to shove she could cope with him knowing how she felt...but did he have to say it out loud?

'Come on,' he urged, 'cough!'

She managed a restrained choke.

'Is it my table manners that offend you?' he suggested jovially. 'Or...?' His brows drew together in a dark straight line as he apparently came up with another interpretation. 'Is it my personal hygiene? Don't be afraid to tell me; I can take it.'

Kat wasn't sure she could. Just thinking about the distinctive male, musky smell of his body made her feel strange and light-headed. The unwanted sexual awareness had infiltrated every cell of her body—the process had taken a single heartbeat.

'*Very funny.* I'm the hired help; this sort of thing—' her

gesture encompassed their elegant surroundings '—makes it look as if I'm being singled out for special treatment.'

'Surely you wouldn't condemn me to my own company,' he taunted gently.

'I wouldn't condemn my worst enemy to your company!' she snapped, taking refuge from frustration in a childish retort.

His spectacular eyes narrowed thoughtful slits. 'Yet you sent Emma to me…'

At the third mention of Emma—Kat had been counting—she felt sick to the stomach. Her relentless imagination had already constructed the wedding scene, with Kat herself walking up the aisle in her bridesmaid dress.

'It was just a figure of speech,' she retorted, uncomfortable.

It hardly mattered what she said, Kat reflected gloomily. Whatever it was, Matt seemed able to turn it back on her.

'You didn't have a problem about sharing my table last night.'

'Last night…'

'Last night Joe came to supper, which meant you could ignore the fact I'm here.'

Kat dropped her fork. His perception was nothing short of scary.

'I'm sorry if you felt left out, but Joe's easy to talk to…' Undemanding, amusing and, most importantly, he didn't inspire any desire to rip off his clothes.

'And you did talk…and talk, and talk…' Matt lifted a languid hand to his mouth to stifle a theatrical yawn.

It was true Kat had felt a need to fill every dangerous silence with a constant stream of light inconsequential chatter.

'The contrast is dramatic. Tonight you've barely opened your mouth.' His willpower wasn't inexhaustible, and his glance flickered hungrily to that tempting orifice. 'And I'm not excluding eating, here.'

'We've already established I'm not about to fade away. I'm simply not hungry.' She was dismayed to discover that what had sounded so coolly dignified in her head had emerged from her mouth sounding appallingly petulant.

'Perhaps I should have invited the lovely Emma to stay...' Matt mused.

Number four!

This was beginning to feel as if he was deliberately rubbing her nose in it... Maybe he didn't like being turned down and this was a sort of 'I've had a better offer' kind of thing.

His dark curling lashes slowly lifted. 'To give you someone to talk to, of course.'

'Why else would you invite a beautiful woman to dinner...?' she agreed nastily with a cynical scowl.

His eyes made a slow deliberate inventory of her curvy figure. The simple dress she wore was one of the cheap but cheerful designer rip-offs that the high street stores did so well these days. Matt had dated women who wore the real thing, but this girl *was* the real thing. The thought came right out of the blue, but he quickly warmed to the theme. She was the sort of woman who made the dress and not the other way around...

'Why, indeed?' he drawled slowly.

Her pulses did uncomfortable things. It was the first time since they'd come to their sort of truce that he'd done anything to signify by look or gesture that he was still aware of her sexually. If she was strictly honest, she had been quite riled by the ease with which he had been controlling his baser instincts, especially when she was being constantly reminded of the struggle she was having with her own.

She tried to look exasperated and not devastated by the slow, sexually loaded scrutiny. It wasn't an easy thing to do when your skin was literally tingling with sexual desire. It was hard to judge from his enigmatic expression how

successful she'd been. She fiddled nervously with the shoe-
string strap of the silky blue dress and tried to calm her
erratic breathing.

'Emma has just been through a nasty divorce,' she began
carefully.

'Are there any other kind?'

The look she shot him would have reduced a more sensitive man to tears... Unfortunately, the only person who
seemed likely to disintegrate at that moment was Kat herself.

'She's rather vulnerable at the moment.' Kat expelled her
breath in an exasperated hiss. Aren't we all? she thought,
giving her head a little shake to clear her foggy thoughts.
'I know she comes over as... But she's not as...' Her
cheeks grew pink as she racked her brains for a tactful way
of explaining away her friend's behaviour.

Matt let her flounder wretchedly for a few moments before coming to her rescue.

'Eager...? Available...?' He raised one eyebrow as Kat
gave a horrified gasp. 'Don't get me wrong, I've no problem as a rule with women who get straight to the point.'

'I just bet you haven't!' she choked. 'How dare you
make assumptions about poor Emma?' she fumed. 'If she
were a man...'

'She isn't.'

For the first time, Kat picked up on the anger he'd been
nursing all evening. It was hard not to shrink back from
the subdued fury in his icy appraisal. The abrupt shift in
his mood intensified her confusion even more.

'Neither is she a physio, as it turns out.'

'Oh!'

'Oh, indeed.'

Nothing could have been more bland than his silkily
smooth smile—it sent an icy shiver up Kat's tense spine.

'I didn't say she was,' Kat defended uneasily.

'No, that's true. I suppose I unreasonably assumed that

a person who was substituting for my physio would be similarly qualified. But then that wasn't the role you wanted a stand-in for, was it, Kathleen...?'.

His words unravelled the last fragile threads of her composure. Was the man a mind-reader or something?

'You're the most arrogant man I've ever met!' The accusation had an uncomfortably pushed-in-a-corner sound to it.

'Perhaps you should have taken her vulnerability and my conceit into account before you set us on a collision course.'

Kat, who had been thinking much the same thing herself, flushed guiltily. She breathed in deeply.

'What do you mean?' she quavered suspiciously.

'Think about it...if you haven't already.' His expression remained bland as Kat's eyes widened in guilty alarm. 'Attractive, recently traumatised young woman, sexually deprived male, very few clothes...is this ringing any bells for you?'

It did; they were all alarm bells. His silkily sensuous words conjured up the hot steamy atmosphere in the pool-house so well that for a moment she didn't really hear them, or understand the implications.

Kat wasn't even aware of getting to her feet and pushing her chair away with hands that were hot and sticky.

'She was doing me a favour.'

The expression of biting scorn in his eyes made her voice die away to a feeble whisper.

'How does that work?' This time there was no mistaking the fact he was in a towering rage. '"If you've got nothing else on could you sleep with this guy for me?"'

'You didn't!' she cried, almost wringing her slim pale hands in distress. 'Emma would have—'

Matt cut across her before she had a chance to utter any further indiscretions.

'Told you all about it? Tell me, do you often compare

notes? How did I score?' he demanded, with an innocent look totally at odds with the crude enquiry.

Kat was too distracted to respond to the gibe. A long tendril of pale hair escaped from her loose chignon as she silently shook her head in mute denial. *What have I done? If Emma does something really daft, like fall in love with him, it'll be my fault!* It was hard for Kat to imagine anyone not falling in love with Matt!

Matt didn't seem in a hurry to put her out of her misery; he seemed to be taking a degree of spiteful relish in her distress.

'And if I did...?' he asked casually.

Her bosom heaved as the colour fled her cheeks. 'I think you're totally despicable!' she announced in a low, contemptuous voice.

'I didn't say I did.'

His flippancy was fresh evidence, if she'd needed any, of his base and callous nature.

'And you didn't say you didn't,' she gritted.

'Never heard of innocent until proven guilty?'

'Never heard of overwhelming circumstantial evidence?' she yelled.

'I was only pointing out what *might* have happened.'

Kat stared at him incredulously. 'You expect me to believe...'

The expression on his face was frostily contemptuous. It wasn't hard to see the steel that had enabled him to carve a niche for himself in an unfriendly business environment.

'I have scruples,' he bit back. 'No, I wouldn't expect you to believe that, Kathleen. It wouldn't suit you at all to believe I have a single redeeming characteristic.'

The accusation had enough truth in it to alarm Kat deeply. 'Don't change the subject,' she insisted defensively.

'You know, I don't quite understand why you're belly-aching. After all, wasn't I *supposed* to be smitten by Emma the svelte and sexy divorcee?'

He couldn't know… It had to be a shot in the dark… didn't it?

'That's a ludicrous thing to say.'

'I can't help but find all this moral superiority a tad hypocritical. What's wrong…did you have second thoughts?'

Again he was bang on target.

'I don't know what you're talking about.'

'You forget, Kathleen, I've been subjected to set-ups by an expert—my mother. In comparison you're merely an inspired amateur, angel.'

'If you and Emma *clicked* it's got nothing to do with me,' she choked hoarsely.

'You could have fooled me.'

If only that were true!

'You hoped I'd be so smitten by your slightly scary Emma I'd forget about kissing you.' Matt got to his feet and the professional Kat automatically registered how much his flexibility had improved, even in the short time she'd been here. The private Kat registered that his smallest gesture just shrieked sex appeal. 'I've news for you, Kathleen,' he added in a soft voice. 'I haven't forgotten!' His steely eyes moved greedily over her softly flushed face.

Kat's shaky composure fragmented totally at the sinfully sensual murmur.

Without considering the consequences of so foolish an action, she allowed her thoughts to drift, along with her wide eyes, in the general direction of his mouth. They were the sort of thoughts that had a taste and texture, and she was filled with a dangerous hunger to sample the real thing.

The outline of his lips suggested passion, but fierce control. Speculating on how hard it would be to make his control slip…just a little…made her legs shake and her mouth grow dry.

A burst of shameful heat travelled over her entire body as she attempted to look away from the blaze of sexual challenge in his half-closed eyes. When she discovered she couldn't, she stuck her chin out and settled for pretending she hadn't heard him.

'Scary...?' she croaked shakily.

The shrewd expression in his hard eyes suggested her diversionary tactics had not gone unnoticed.

'I'm not too keen on being manipulated.' The direct look he shot her made Kat drop her eyes self-consciously; the subtext of that look had been painfully obvious. 'And I rather think your Emma has her own reasons for playing the *femme fatale*...' he mused thoughtfully.

Femme fatale? Kat's head lifted; her eyes were wide and indignant. Just what had Emma been up to...? So much for best friend's lovers being out of bounds!

'I'm sure some blokes get an extra buzz from the danger factor of a jealous husband in the background...only I'm not one of them.'

'Luc is history,' Kat responded with a puzzled look. 'They're divorced.'

His broad shoulders lifted. 'Maybe.'

'They *are* divorced,' she insisted.

'I'm not disputing that.'

'Then what are you disputing?'

'The history part. I got the impression...' He gave an irritated frown. 'You know, I'm not all that interested in Emma—or her husband.'

Nervous tension made Kat more candid than she might otherwise have been. 'Well, you must have acted like you were interested,' she observed tartly, 'to make Em so keen,' she elaborated indiscreetly.

His expression grew satirical. 'Must be my natural charm.'

'How can you laugh?' she cried angrily. 'She might get hurt.'

'I think you're overrating my irresistibility,' he came back drily. 'Or maybe you find it hard to be objective where I'm concerned.'

Kat gave a horrified gasp, frantic to escape. Her enthusiasm made her clumsy; her heel caught on the hem of her dress, she grabbed at the chair, and for a moment she swayed precariously before her balance deserted her completely and she went down heavily, taking her chair with her. One solid oak leg hit her a glancing blow on the head as it fell with an even louder clatter to the floor.

Hand on her head, she opened her eyes to find Matt leaning over her, his dark face taut with concern.

'I don't think I broke it,' she mumbled stupidly.

'Broke what?' He pulled away her hand and scrutinised the discoloured area it had hidden on her temple.

'The chair.' With her luck, it was probably a wildly expensive antique.

Matt looked at her incredulously for a moment.

'God, you're serious, aren't you?' A sliver of dull colour ran under his skin and seeped along the bitingly perfect line of his slanted, sharply delineated cheekbones. 'To hell with the chair!'

Kat couldn't approve of such a cavalier attitude to someone else's property. If the world hadn't been spinning so horridly she would have told him. She closed her eyes. The spinning didn't stop but mercifully it did slow.

She felt firm, cool, *gentle* fingers against her skin, and any slight inclination she had to move faded. The gentle component of his touch made her throat thicken emotionally. 'What do they say—you can run but you can't hide…?'

Trite, she mused—oblivious to the fact she'd spoken out loud—and over-used, but very appropriate for this situation. Even if she had succeeded in running away from Matt, there was no running away from her feelings for him. To cut a short story even shorter, she'd fallen for him big-time!

'You've taken quite a bash on the head.' She felt her long skirts being neatly rearranged over her exposed legs. 'Does it hurt anywhere else? Don't move…!' His seductive tones deepened to a disapproving growl as she began to struggle into a sitting position.

'I'm fine now,' Kat insisted, batting away his restraining hand.

She finally realised that Matt was beside her, kneeling on his right knee with the other leg extended to the side. She knew without asking that this was a wildly uncomfortable position for him to be in.

'Be careful!' she cried. 'You shouldn't be...' she began, her eyes widening in alarm. She pulled herself onto her own knees and placed both hands protectively on his injured leg. 'That was so stupid, Matt.' Her slender fingers slid anxiously over his thigh, and lower, until, finding no obvious signs of damage, she gave a sigh of relief.

About the same time she stopped worrying that he'd done himself harm being noble and silly, Kat started being aware of a lot of other things—things like the tension in the long firm muscles under her fingers; things like Matt's audible respirations, fast and shallow. The dragging sensation low in her belly intensified until she could hardly bear it. She heard the low wispy little moan without being conscious of it coming from her own mouth.

'You should be more cautious.' It occurred to her that asking Matt to be cautious was just as futile as asking an earthquake to be gentle; there was something elemental about them both. 'You could have hurt yourself.'

The reproach had a soft insubstantial sound to it as if it, like herself, could have been blown away by a stray puff of wind. There was no air stirring in the room; the stillness had a strange, heavy, expectant quality.

'I didn't, but you did.'

There was no legitimate reason for her to touch him now, but Kat was experiencing a strange reluctance to break the contact. It felt as if neat electricity was entering her body. The entry point could be traced back to the point where her tingling fingertips were in contact with his body.

'I'm fine.' Kat wasn't sure if this was true. She felt strange...very strange. It couldn't be concussion because that didn't extend beyond your head, and her strange feeling involved her toes too, and for that matter all points in between the two!

Using the powerful muscles of his right leg, Matt heaved himself to his feet in one fluid motion. The abrupt movement left Kat draped up against him.

'Be careful,' she scolded a little belatedly as he drew up to his full height. The surging movement had drawn her pliant body upwards too, until her face was pressed against the strong manly curve of his thigh. The words 'compromising position' popped into her head. 'If anyone walked in now...'

'What would they think, Kathleen?' he asked, his tone imperative. His fingers closed firmly around her jaw and tilted her face up to him.

Mutely she stared into the charismatic glow of his eyes and shook her head.

That unique, exciting, combustible quality of his had never been more apparent. His eyes held more *life* than she'd thought it possible for one person to contain. His vitality was almost a living force in its own right...she was drawn to it as inexorably as a moth to a flame.

God, but he takes my breath away!

His fingers came slowly up to her mouth and very carefully he began to trace the curve of her slightly parted lips. She didn't consciously open her mouth and invite a deeper, more intimate exploration—it just happened.

Reading the longing in her wide eyes, Matt slid the tip of his forefinger just inside the cushiony softness of her upper lip; he felt her catch her breath. An abbreviated grunt escaped the confines of his deep chest when Kat's tongue darted out to touch his finger.

From that moment the exploration escalated rapidly to the point where she had hold of his wrist and was alternately suckling greedily on his fingers and pressing hard damp kisses to his wrist and the palm of his hand.

Up to that moment in her life, compulsion had just been a word like any other to Kat; now she was consumed by it.

She let out a tiny cry of annoyance when Matt's free hand slid into her hair and jerked her head backwards.

Kat's eyes swept hungrily over his starkly handsome face. The intriguing planes and sharp angles of his face were enhanced by the fine sheen of sweat that had broken out over his skin. He really did have a bone structure that was to die for, she thought, storing away the image of his strong slashing cheekbones and wide sensual mouth in her memory. She didn't want to forget a single detail of how he looked at that moment!

His burning eyes lifted with difficulty from the heaving outline of her bosom as it strained against the modestly cut bodice of her dress. Her face didn't offer any respite from the explosive sexual excitement that was building up inside him. He dwelt for a long moment on her succulent parted, trembling lips and passion-glazed eyes; the wild, wanton expression on her beautiful flushed face was the sort of thing male fantasies were made of. That expression screamed out bold, unambiguous surrender.

When he spoke, his voice was thick. 'Do you have any idea of what you're doing to me?' he demanded hoarsely.

Matt had always prided himself on being a considerate, controlled lover, who always put his partner's pleasure before his own. So what went wrong, man? he asked himself, struggling with a primitive urge to push her onto the table and...

Anyhow, as daft questions went, this was up there with the best of them. *Did she know...?* Hell, from where she was kneeling it would have been hard to miss! He firmly closed the door on that line of thought. He was having enough trouble getting his more basic impulses under control without dwelling on the erotic possibilities of her position.

The sly, clever, circular movement of her slim fingers in
an upwards direction tended to confirm his suspicions. Attack and retreat, attack and retreat, the tormenting cycle
went on and on… Her passion-glazed eyes never left his
all the time her busy fingers were at work.

Kat's lips curved in a satisfied sultry smile; she felt as if
she were burning up from the inside out.

'Don't you want me to…?' she wondered dreamily. If
he said no, she'd just have to persuade him to change his
mind. At that moment, she had complete faith in her powers
of persuasion… Surrender was an unexpectedly empowering experience.

Her breath was coming in short, frantic little gasps. The
anticipation levels inside her were building to unimaginable
levels, but she still pushed it, impelled by something she
didn't understand to test the limits of his control and her
own. She discovered Matt's limit at about the same time
her fingers discovered the hard ridge that pushed against
the restrictions of his well-cut pants. Experimentally, her
hand closed over him; intense excitement bubbled up inside
her as the throbbing erection pushed back against her
cupped hand.

She hardly registered the pain in her scalp as his fingers
tightened convulsively. She began to be alarmed when his
head fell backwards. She watched as the corded sinews of
his strong neck stood out sharply against his heated skin.
He looked like a man in agony. Oh, God, what have I done?

'Sorry!' she gasped pulling her hand away. 'Did I hurt
you?' she asked miserably.

Mortification washed over her in a great tide. How could
I…? she wondered, reviewing her wanton behaviour with
a sense of disbelief. But even while she was considering
her disgraceful behaviour, the ache in her treacherous body
intensified. The pain involved her entire body, but it was

concentrated in specific areas; the worst affected were her tender swollen breasts and the apex between her thighs.

'Hurt!' he echoed, his voice warmly incredulous.

Kat gave a startled little cry as one strong hand curled around her waist and lifted her bodily to her feet. The other was equally firm about replacing her own hand against his glorious arousal.

'I can take quite a bit of that kind of hurt.' He thrust his hips forward to seal their lower bodies together, trapping her hand firmly between them.

'Really!'

Something inside Matt moved; the unidentifiable feeling couldn't be classified as lust alone. Matt worked on instinct... He wasn't into navel-gazing and self-analysis, so he didn't pause to wonder about the cause of the new feeling.

The sense of wonder in her voice, the blush on her smooth cheeks; they both sent his thoughts—his brain was still functioning at a *basic* level—in an unexpected direction. He dismissed the fleeting notion out of hand; it just wasn't possible, he reasoned.

His mouth was just inches from her own. Kat waited for his kiss with eager, breathless anticipation. Even breathing was an irritating distraction, all her senses were tuned into what was going to come next. On tiptoes, she stretched upwards eagerly as his dark head bent forward.

'Oh, God...*yes*...!' Kat moaned deeply as his lips found hers.

It only took a few moments for the initial voluptuous leisurely exploration to be transformed into a fevered contest to increase the intimacy of the contact. Teeth grazing, tongues exploring, the erotic duel continued until both combatants broke off, panting for breath.

Kat wondered if she looked as stunned and shaken as Matt did as he looked down into her face; she suspected she did.

'You said you wouldn't kiss me,' she reminded him in a voice that sounded unfamiliar to her own ears.

'What can I say? I lied. I suppose I might as well be hung for a sheep as a lamb.'

Kat closed her eyes and gave a rapturous sigh of anticipation as his dark head swooped downwards to capture his target.

When he lifted his head, Kat was having trouble standing upright.

'There only seems one thing left for me to say.' His expression didn't quite match the flippancy of his husky tone. 'Your place or mine...?'

This was the moment she ought to deliver some stinging retort and make a fast escape. Instead, Kat asked herself if the transitory pleasure of sleeping with this man was worth losing her job and facing a financially insecure future. She looked deep into his heart-stopping blue orbs... *You bet it was!*

'You don't give up.' The man was relentless...*thank heaven!*

'Do you want me to?' he asked, without the suggestion of a smile; the smile came when she shook her head in fervent denial.

To hell with etiquette, references, or job security! There was no way Kat was going to reject what he was offering her. How could she when there was every chance that she'd never feel this way again in her life? In fact, if anyone had tried to stop her accepting what he was offering, the ensuing tussle would have involved a lot of kicking and screaming.

'Yours seems the more sensible choice.' Anxious not to come over as gauche and naïve, Kat tried to act as if she had discussions like this every day of the week. 'I'm on the second floor,' she reminded him.

'I love it when you're practical.'

'Talking of practical,' she replied, regarding the elaborate table with misgivings, 'won't it cause a few raised eyebrows if we leave in the middle of the meal?'

'It'll cause a whole lot more than a few raised eyebrows if I don't get you somewhere private fast,' he growled. 'Get the picture…?'

Kat brushed a strand of sweat-dampened hair from her eyes. When she moved, her dress clung damply to her skin—she did get the picture.

'Don't forget your cane.' A deep-seated protective instinct took over at this point and made her lower her eyes from his. She knew what she was feeling was reflected on her face.

'What do I need a cane for when I have you?' He slipped one arm lightly over her shoulders. She was startled to hear him say, 'See how I need you…'

It could be she was reading something into his words that wasn't there… On the other hand… Kat's gaze moved from his fingertips all the way up his arm and then naturally to his face. There was nothing to confirm or deny her speculation in his taut expression. She found she couldn't— didn't want to—run away from his scrutiny this time.

One dark brow rose. 'Ready, Kathleen…?' he asked softly.

Unconsciously she straightened her shoulders. She slid her arm around his narrow waist. She took a fortifying lungful of air. 'It's now or never!' she declared courageously.

Matt blinked, his lip curled in a self-derisive smile. He couldn't recall anyone ever acting as though sharing his bed was on par with root canal work. Matt wondered why he still expected this girl to say what he expected; he felt his ire dissolve as she raised her questioning eyes to his face… She was so damned beautiful.

CHAPTER SEVEN

THE moment the bedroom door closed behind them Kat withdrew her support and slid sinuously from under his arm. After their unexpected and painfully embarrassing encounter with Elizabeth Nichols in the hallway, her caring disposition was in tatters. She wouldn't have shed a tear at that particular moment if Matt had fallen on his beautiful, lying face—in fact it would have been a plus-point!

He did nothing so inelegant of course.

'How could you?' she breathed, pressing her hands to her burning cheeks.

'How could I what?'

His aggravating pretence of ignorance made her grind her even white teeth; the sound was audible enough to make Matt wince.

'Don't come the blue-eyed innocent with me, Matthew Devlin.' She planted her hands firmly on her hips and impatiently shook a stray hank of heavy blonde hair from her eyes.

'Don't come the nanny from hell with me, Kathleen Wray.' The warning note in his deep voice was the final straw for Kat. 'I'm an easy-going man...' Whilst he paused to allow her shrill incredulous laughter to die away, Matt demonstrated his easy-going nature by glaring at her with smouldering disapproval.

'Some blokes would have cut up rough when you sent in a substitute kisser. Just try and remember there are limits to my tolerance.'

But not, it seemed to his brass-faced gall!

'"Don't worry, Mrs Nichols,"' she trilled in a sing-song voice. '"*Kathleen* knows exactly what I need."' Actually,

123

Kathleen had been worried to death at that point she wasn't adequate to the task, but she wasn't about to explain that to him.

'Actually, I like to think I'm more of a bass baritone than a soprano,' he drawled provocatively.

Kat let out a subdued wail. He seemed determined to treat this as a joke. 'Why didn't you just draw her a diagram?'

'Which part did you have a problem with? The bit where I admitted I was in pain…'

Kat clutched her head in her hands. 'Don't remind me!' she pleaded.

'Or the part where I explained I was in need of urgent treatment? It would seem,' he murmured, adopting an aggravating, much ill-used tone, 'that I can't do right as far as you're concerned. You were the one who told me I should admit it when I'm in pain,' he pointed out in a voice that suggested she was being unreasonable.

'You know full well that when I said that I was referring to your stupid macho posturing, not *that* sort of pain.'

'Only you and I, angel, know what sort of pain I was talking about.' His eyes were openly caressing as they ran over her face, and lower, over the womanly curves of her splendid body.

'It shows a lack of respect for someone who has known you since you were a child!' she ranted self-righteously. 'You were laughing at her.'

Annoyance flickered over his face. 'Actually, I was laughing at you.' It was hard to miss the fact he wasn't any longer. 'I think we've already established I'm a callous, selfish bastard, Kathleen. So if you're looking for a reason to walk through that door, you've got an excuse on tap. There's no need for all this drama.' He gestured towards the closed door. 'If you want to walk, be my guest.' He extracted the key and held it out towards her.

It was matter of self-respect that he didn't show how

much he didn't want her to take him up on his offer. Despite this, he held his breath during the painful pause that followed.

'I want to stay here.' Her wide eyes flickered almost fearfully to his uncompromising face. 'With you.'

Well, why do you think he imagines you want to stay, girl? she asked herself crossly. To admire the décor? Still, you've managed to clear up any uncertainty on the subject; now he *knows* you're besotted!

'Good.'

Is that all he has to say? I've just offered myself up on a platter and he says, *Good!* Her bosom was swelling with a deep sense of misuse when Matt took a step towards her. Kat didn't realise until the last second what he intended to do.

With a gentle tug at the stretchy fabric of her dress, he inserted the key neatly between her breasts. As his fingertips brushed against her skin the key was swallowed up by the twin mounds of firm creamy flesh.

'Just so that we both know where it is should either of us change our mind.'

The eroticism of the gesture was just too much to take. Kat drew a painful shaky breath. There was a liquid warmness in the pit of her stomach and it was spreading... She gazed back at him, almost paralysed with lust, and discovered Matt's gaze hadn't made it beyond the outline of her brazenly distended nipples.

She couldn't even take the faltering couple of steps backwards without being reminded that her physical arousal extended beyond her burning nipples. She was painfully conscious of the treacherous wetness between her legs as she moved. The cold metal between her breasts was losing its chill against her hot skin.

What had happened to the young woman who had walked into this house emotionally well balanced? Shielded from the excesses of the mating game by strong principles

and high moral standards. How was it possible to want a
man so much?

The back of her knees hit the bed...*his* bed. Someone
had turned it down... The sight of the crisp cotton sheets
made Kat's out-of-control stomach muscles tighten another
painful notch. She automatically avoided the business end
of the bed—it just seemed a shame to spoil those pristine,
unsullied sheets—and sat down heavily on the edge.

'You shouldn't have said those things to her,' she persisted in a fretful tone. 'I've never been so embarrassed.'
With a distracted sigh, she let her high-heeled sandals slip
one by one to the floor.

Matt watched as she rubbed one set of pearly painted
nails against the instep of her opposing foot.

'Lighten up, Kat,' he suggested indulgently. He wondered if it wouldn't be such a bad idea if he followed his
own advice. Any male, barring those with legitimate foot
fetishes, who was driven to distraction by the sight of a
pretty ankle was getting way too intense!

The more laid back Matt got, the more uptight she felt
and acted.

'*Lighten up?*' she echoed. '*Lighten up?*' It was Matt's
turn to look pained as her voice rose shrilly. 'My God, I'd
have been perfectly justified if I'd walked out of here and
left you...'

'*Aching?*'

At the sound of his throaty interjection her eyelids flickered upwards his expression was frustratingly enigmatic.

'I think we've already established you don't want to
leave, Kathleen.'

'Aching?' she echoed in a shocked voice. '*Really?*'

Oh, God, why don't I just go write a sign across my
forehead saying 'needy and pathetic'? *Cringeworthy, or
what?* Is this really me, so desperate to please a man...?

To her relief, Matt's expression didn't suggest her behaviour was in any way unusual.

'Actually, Kathleen, I was being quite restrained. You ever seen a grown man cry like a baby?' he added, in case she had missed the point he was trying to make.

Torn between tears and laughter, she felt her mobile lips wobble. 'You don't cry,' she sniffed.

'I can learn. In fact, I've been meaning to get in touch with my feminine side for some time now. On second thoughts, that might not be such a good idea... You might not believe this but I was mistaken for someone of the gay persuasion quite recently.'

Gnawing anxiously on her lower lip, Kat drew her knees up under her chin and, resting her chin on the shelf they formed, glared resentfully up at his perfect profile from under the dark curling sweep of her lashes.

'All right, there's no need to rub it in.'

It still embarrassed Kat no end that she'd assumed on such fragile evidence that the most rampantly *male* male she'd ever encountered was gay! Perhaps on some subconscious level her eagerness to embrace this preposterous conclusion had been partly due to her own reluctance to admit, even to herself, the effect he had had on her from the very first moment.

'I think there's every need. When a man has been traumatised the way I was...'

Kat hooted derisively. 'Sure, you look very traumatised.'

Trauma she could deal with; heart-stopping gorgeousness was another matter. Have I fallen in love with a pretty face...? No, it was more than that...*much* more than that.

Matt inclined his head in smooth acknowledgement of the accusation. His magnificent shoulders lifted as he limped slowly but inexorably towards her.

Kat noisily cleared the congestion in her throat.

'They're probably all gossiping about us now. You weren't exactly subtle,' she babbled nervously.

'You, on the other hand, looked like a kid who'd been caught with her hand in the cookie jar.'

Her eyes made a swift head-to-toe survey of his tall rangy frame; she stifled an appreciative sigh—just. Some cookie...*some man!* Desire clawed deep inside and Kat licked her dry lips nervously.

'You looked so damned guilty, I couldn't resist,' he admitted huskily.

'You were obviously one of those little boys who spent many a long hour watching twitching flies expire!' she complained, without all that much conviction. Privately, she thought Matt must have been a delicious little boy...

A dreamy expression drifted across her face. His sons would no doubt be equally appealing... Her eyes widened in alarm as she swiftly brought this line of speculation to an abrupt halt.

'What does it matter if she knows?'

Kat realised that, as unlikely as it seemed, his bewilderment was totally genuine. She sniffed angrily and twitched restively at the thin shoulder-strap which insisted on crawling down her arm.

'You might not care what people think...'

'You catch on fast...' he admired with restrained sarcasm.

'But I do!' she told him forcefully. Well, it was *meant* to be a forceful condemnation; what actually emerged from her painfully dry, aching throat was a whisper—a forceful whisper, but nonetheless a whisper.

'Why? It's a total waste of energy to worry about what other people think of you,' he explained, delivering one of his ruthless charismatic smiles.

He made it sound so simple, and she supposed for him it was. 'Easy for you to say,' she snapped.

'You should try it,' he recommended casually.

'A nice philosophy but not exactly practical. Most of us ordinary mortals don't have your giant ego,' she pointed out spikily.

The closer he got, the harder it got for her to concentrate

on what he was saying. She felt a flare of panic when she did manage to decipher the words that were emerging from his achingly beautiful mouth.

'Maybe you should be more concerned about what I think…?'

'There seem to be plenty of folk anxious to jump when you click your fingers already!' she observed disapprovingly.

'I don't snap my fingers.'

'No, you just smile.'

He looked taken aback by the ferocity of her response. 'You have a problem with my smile?'

A bigger one than you could ever suspect!

Matt's expression grew impatient when she didn't respond. 'If you carry on like this, I'll start to think you're ashamed of sharing my bed.'

'Maybe I am.'

The consequences of what she was about to do were far-reaching. Even if she put aside the emotional aspect of taking a lover whose only commitment was to pleasure— a lover, furthermore, she was desperately in love with— there was the fact she was about to sleep herself out of a job when her financial situation was dire.

His blue eyes grew cold with displeasure. Kat got the full force of that icy look and stubbornly swallowed the retraction which had sprung to her lips. How dared he glare at her that way?

'Have you had a change of heart somewhere between the door and the bed…?'

Good question, Kat.

'Is that what this is about?' he persisted.

Kat had no idea what he was driving at.

His deep-set eyes were hard and expressionless as he scanned her face, but despite the aloof exterior Kat had the impression he'd mind a lot if she *had* changed her mind… Even the suggestion made her foolish heart soar.

It seemed an appropriate time for a brutal reminder. This was sex, plain and simple, and there was absolutely no excuse for her to dress it up as anything else. If this was going to happen, it was imperative she didn't try and kid herself it meant anything deep and meaningful to Matt. In the long run it would be less painful, she told herself dully.

Matt was the one who seemed to feel the need to fill the lengthening silence.

'I realise that most men you sleep with don't need your support, quite literally, to get you into bed.' His laughter held no humour as his eyes left her face to flicker downwards over his left leg. As his fingertips brushed against his thigh, his brooding expression conveyed a deep contempt for his own weakness. 'But once I get horizontal I expect I'll be able to give you value for money.'

It wasn't the crudeness of his boast that brought the guttural sound of indignant denial to her lips, but rather the ridiculous and deeply insulting notion that she gave a damn about his injury.

'That remains to be seen,' she responded in a clear, confident voice.

As a cure for incipient self-pity, her bracing comment seemed to have done the trick. He looked at her with startled shock that was on the point of tipping over into indulgent amusement. Kat didn't bother disguising the fact she felt smugly pleased she'd succeeded in surprising him.

She knew that if she wanted to scold him some more she'd have to be quick about it; once he grinned at her in that crinkly blue-eyed way she'd be as stern as marshmallow.

'Since when,' she demanded self-righteously, 'was making love all about fitness levels?' Since when did I become such an expert...? 'Making love,' she added knowledgeably, 'isn't about staying power. And you don't have to be a contortionist to get it right.' At least, I hope not.

Matt was staring at her in a fascinated fashion.

'True,' he replied gravely, 'but I hope you won't deny that neither do any harm.' Under the satirical glare of his deep-set eyes, Kat blushed deeply. 'Call me over-sensitive, but have I done something to make you mad?'

'Beyond imply I'm shallow and silly enough to care about your scars, *not a thing*,' she gritted acidly. 'It's not like I'd be seeing anything I haven't seen before.'

'What, *nothing*! Why, Kathleen, I'm shocked you peeked!' he chided.

'I didn't!' she squeaked.

Matt's expression sobered before she could embarrass herself any more. 'Whatever you've seen, Kathleen, you've seen it clinically.' His faith in her willpower made Kat shift uneasily... If he knew the half of it! 'Seeing it as a lover would be quite different.'

Hearing him refer to them as lovers sent a sharp thrill zinging through her body.

'That's what I'm hoping,' she responded boldly. 'As for your stamina, how do you know I wouldn't prefer you weak and at my mercy...?'

His smokily blue eyes glowed dangerously. 'Guilty on both counts.'

'Don't be flippant.'

'I'm not. Besides, you're right.'

'I am?' Deflated, she stared back at him in a baffled, uneasy kind of way.

'Beautiful women curled up on my bed are always right,' he explained simply.

It was nothing but a slick meaningless nothing, the sort of patter he used when seducing the endless stream of women who occupied his bed on a temporary basis. Something inside her rebelled noisily. She didn't want to be the same as the others; she wanted this to be different!

'Don't try and s-soft soap me, Matthew Devlin,' she stuttered. Despite her protest, anticipation fluttered hotly deep in her belly. 'Oh, God!' she gasped suddenly.

Matt saw her eyes snap open, wide and contrite.

'You're not worried, are you…?' She lowered her voice to a subdued whisper. 'That you might not be able…that you can't…?' She coloured as she fished about clumsily for the words least likely to wound a delicate masculine ego. 'Because if you are I'd be just as happy with a hug,' she reassured him earnestly.

Matt let out a great shout of laughter that seemed to indicate her concerns were unfounded. He planted his hands on her shoulders to steady himself before he bent forward to kiss her in a masterly fashion on her parted lips. He drew her upwards and forward in such a manner that made it impossible for her not to notice his libido was in good working order.

By the time his dark head had lifted, Kat's head was spinning dizzily. She sank back down onto the bed like a limp rag doll and pressed the back of her shaking hand to her swollen lips.

'Happy with a hug…?' He seemed to find this the best joke he'd heard in ages. 'You're a delicious little liar.'

'I am not!' She felt obliged to protest, even though she liked the sound of that 'delicious'.

'Are too.' He displayed obvious pleasure at being offered the chance to echo her childish retort. 'Don't get me wrong, hugs are good in their own way, but I want much more than a hug from you. And we both know you'd be about as satisfied with a hug as I would be,' he accused. 'I appreciate your concern, but I think you might have taken a throwaway comment too much to heart. I don't think I'd be the only man who didn't feel particularly randy while he was recovering from multiple fractures.'

This wasn't the sort of house where the bedsprings squeaked, so when Matt lowered his long lean frame onto the bed beside her there was nothing but silence, acres of dense, nerve-stretching silence.

'And it wasn't soft soap.' His fingers closed firmly

around her chin. 'You are beautiful, and this is my bed.' He wouldn't permit her to evade his searching eyes.

Even if she'd wanted to dispute either of those facts, she couldn't have; what Kat saw in his eyes made her insides dissolve.

Matt ran a single finger softly over the lovely angle of her jaw. He felt her quiver and his eyes darkened. 'And I've been thinking about getting you into it—' his hand pressed against the mattress '—since almost the first moment I set eyes on you. This was always inevitable, you know, Kathleen,' he purred persuasively.

Kat didn't need persuading. 'Inevitable as in I'd be a push-over?'

She gave a small, self-derisive smile which turned into a tiny shriek as he placed one hand square on her chest and pushed her over in the literal sense.

'Gosh! I'm a fallen woman.' Despite the benign nature of her fall, Kat felt as breathless as if she'd just bungee-jumped from a ten-storey building.

His low laughter was warm and caressing. 'That sounds promising...'

The smile died from her lips. 'It is,' she told him huskily. Their eyes locked and neither smiled.

Without saying a word he took hold of her legs underneath the knees and swivelled her fully onto the bed. There was a flattering urgency about his actions.

It didn't occur to Kat to tell him not to exert himself; he seemed to know exactly what he was doing. It's probably just as well one of us does, she reflected, stifling a surge of uneasiness.

Heart pounding, she lay there passive and pliant as he planted a hand either side of her head and stretched out beside her.

An expression of wonder in her eyes, Kat reached up and let her fingers drift featherlight over his lean face. Matt turned his head and kissed the palm of her cupped hand.

'You really are quite, quite beautiful,' she breathed with husky reverence. It was a confession she'd been aching to make; Kat found the experience remarkably liberating.

A smile that was tender and at the same time ferocious curved his lips in response. 'A somewhat battered beauty...?' His hand went to the scar on his cheek.

'I want to kiss the scars, all of them,' she announced dreamily.

'Is that so?' He extended the kiss from her palm all the way down the inner aspect of her slim arm in a series of soft feathery kisses until he came to the delicate blue-veined area of her wrist.

He groaned and pressed his face into her open hand. 'You have absolutely no idea what's it's been like having you touch and yet not touch me, if you know what I mean.'

Kat knew *exactly* what he meant. She looked at the back of his dark head and was swamped by a mixture of feelings that ranged from outright predatory to a tenderness that bordered on the protective. Despite the wild contrast, she didn't feel any conflict; she'd never felt anything in her life that felt this right.

She ran her hand over the curve of his strong back, feeling the responsive quiver of tight, taut muscles as she did so. When the feelings got too raw to bear, she buried her face in his shoulder and eagerly drank in the warm, intimate, very male scent of his aroused body.

'Me too!' she whispered fiercely as he rolled onto his side and took her with him.

His hand slid smoothly under the slippery fabric of her dress. Kat caught her breath as his fingers touched her skin; the contact was electrifying.

'Your skin is so soft,' he rasped thickly as his hand glided smoothly over the warm skin of her calf.

By the time his fingers had reached her thigh, Kat was gasping noisily for breath. When they slid under the lacy hem of her knickers and touched the silky fuzz between her legs, she cried out loud at the shocking intimacy.

'You don't like that?' Matt knew she did; he was just greedy to hear her say it.

'I do! I do!'

Her heavy eyelids lifted and she found his cerulean eyes were fixed unblinkingly on her flushed face. Kat swallowed; there was something raw and basic in the taut, driven expression on his face.

Tears welled in her eyes; she was literally drowning in a sensual sea of sensation. 'Don't stop!' she pleaded.

Desperate to be closer to him, she shuffled her body sinuously forward until they were virtually joined at the hip. She squirmed some more as she felt the hard ridge of his arousal grind against her sensitive pelvis.

Their eyes locked and the sexual tension became so heavy she didn't dare breathe. Without losing eye contact, she lifted her leg and hooked it over his narrow waist, effectively locking him against her.

That wasn't the only thing it did. A deep growl vibrated in Matt's chest as he felt her hot, moist, feminine sweetness open up for him. He slid one finger forward over her slick wetness and touched the tight nub of flesh.

Kat just dissolved inside.

Matt watched as her head fell backwards. A shudder shivered up his spine when the keening note emerged from her open mouth. Eyes blazing, Matt bent forward and drove his tongue deep inside her mouth.

His wickedly lustful tongue and lips didn't let up their onslaught, not even for a second. Kat was swept along on the dizzying tide of his hot desire. All the time he sucked and bit, his fingers were stroking the aching core of her until she felt she'd die from sheer pleasure. Somewhere along the way Kat surrendered control with a feeling of joyous release.

Just when she thought she couldn't take any more, he stopped.

Kat was lying on top of him by this point; her dress was rucked up around her waist, revealing a lot of creamy thigh and the suggestion of a firm, femininely rounded bottom. Matt burrowed his dark head into the pillow and pressed his nose up against the side of hers; their breath mingled. Kat's teeth were clenched; she was shaking feverishly. Deep tremors shook Matt's entire body intermittently.

'Tell me you want me, Kathleen.'

That was easy. Kat was almost disappointed that his request wasn't tougher. She was completely consumed by a burning desire to prove herself and her love, if not by word but by deed. She'd prove she'd do anything for him, absolutely anything to please him; she couldn't wait for the opportunity to demonstrate this willingness. Part of her was terrified by the level of commitment, and part of her revelled in the erotic possibilities.

'I want you, Matt.'

Matt's eyes were closed, but his deep sigh had a smugly satisfied sound to it. He sat up and, loosening his tie, pulled it over his head. Still straddled across his knees, Kat had no option but to sit up too.

Holding her eyes, he flicked open the top button of his shirt. A nerve was pulsing spasmodically in his lean cheek; he was close enough for her to feel the fragrant warmth of his uneven breath across her cheeks, close enough for her to appreciate the fine even texture of his skin, close enough for her to be racked with a searing need to touch him—she did.

As she placed her hand flat on his belly she felt the sharp contraction of tight firm muscles beneath her splayed fingers; a tiny mewing sound of pleasure emerged from between her parted lips.

Eyes demurely downcast, tongue tucked firmly between her white teeth, she flicked him a sultry teasing look. A languorous sigh caused her aching breasts to strain tightly against the lightly boned bodice of her dress.

Matt's eyes followed the rapid undulating motion; his scrutiny inflicted further damage to her breathing. With agonising slowness, he began to slide one narrow strap over her shoulder. When the strap hung loose, he began to turn his attention to the remaining one.

He didn't seem to have any trouble locating the zip down the back of her dress. When gravity didn't immediately oblige him he gave it a helping hand and peeled the soft fabric back until her breasts were revealed.

The key fell forgotten to the floor. There was a sibilant hiss of indrawn breath. The blood rushed to her cheeks and, without thinking, she raised her hands to cover herself. Shaking his head, Matt caught her wrists and firmly drew her arms away.

'Never...never...' he reproached huskily. 'Dear, sweet...but you're incredible.' His half-closed eyes gleamed as they followed the gentle sway of her pink-tipped breasts.

Kat's momentary doubts fell away; her mood soared to dizzying wanton heights.

'Touch me.' Her words were half plea, half defiant challenge.

With a groan Matt buried his face in her breasts; he drank in the scent and softness of her with the desperation of a starving man. She felt his hand curve around one aching breast, felt him take the weight of it before he slowly drew the engorged peak into his mouth.

Kat's back arched and her mouth opened in a soundless moan. Her head fell backwards; the urgent motion sent the last of her hairpins adrift, leaving the pale silky tresses to flow unrestricted to midway between her shoulderblades. She couldn't speak; she could hardly breathe! His attentions shifted to the neglected breast. Her nipples burnt with pleasure; the ache deep in her belly grew almost unbearable in its intensity.

'Please!' she begged brokenly, twisting her fingers tight in his thick wavy hair. 'I want you to love me, Matt, please...!'

Matt lifted his head. There was dark flush along the crest of his cheekbones; his eyes were dark and strangely unfocused. For a moment Kat felt a flare of fear—he looked like a stranger—then as he continued to stare down into her face the blank, carnal expression faded.

'Just try and stop me...' he growled, pushing her down across the bed, only pausing to rip off his shirt with flattering urgency before he joined her. 'That is to say,' he corrected himself with a frown, 'you could stop me...*just*. But, hell, you're not going to, are you...?'

Kat gazed across at him with open adoration. 'That's not an option at this stage,' she told him huskily.

'You have no idea how glad I am to hear you say that.'

Kat lifted herself up on one elbow and pushed a hank of long blonde hair from her face; her skin was damp, her breathing one step away from hyperventilation. Boldly she reached across and ran a hand all the way down the leanly muscled torso.

Eyes dark and smoky with desire, Matt reached for his belt buckle.

Kat shook her head. She bent over and kissed him deeply. 'I want to,' she explained huskily when they eventually parted.

With a tiny nod of assent Matt rolled onto his back. One arm curved above his head, his eyes half-closed, he watched her fumble with the belt and zip. He only got occasional glimpses of her face; her long hair hid it from view.

The zip slid down and he heard her startled intake of breath. His self-control snapped.

'Sorry, but this is torture.' He slid his legs over the side of the bed. Two seconds later he was back beside her, naked and marvellously aroused.

Kat stared; she couldn't help herself.

'Touch me, Kathleen.'

Kat gulped and raised her eyes with difficulty. 'I'd like to, only I don't want to do anything wrong.'

'Wrong...?'

'The thing is, you see...' She screwed her eyes up tight—this was *so* embarrassing. 'I've never actually done this before.'

There was a long disbelieving silence, during which Kat's feelings of inadequacy were multiplying by leaps and bounds.

'Are you trying to tell me,' he began in an odd voice, 'that you're a...a...'

Kat sighed. 'Virgin,' she admitted gloomily. Elbow crooked, she anchored her hair off her face and gazed over at him. 'Perhaps I shouldn't have mentioned it.'

Matt swallowed. 'Oh, you should have,' he assured her throatily. And I probably shouldn't ask this, he thought, asking anyhow, 'Why me?'

She almost told him.

'I must have been waiting for the best.'

Kat felt relieved when a slow smile spread over his face; he had been looking pretty grim since she'd fessed up.

'How,' he asked, drawing her towards him, 'can you know something's the best if you've no room for comparison?'

'I'll know.'

'You nervous, angel?' He kissed her softly on the lips.

Her eyes, wide and trusting, melded with his. 'Not with you.'

The muscles in his flat belly contracted sharply as he gasped. Eyes aflame, he nuzzled the sides of her mouth before sliding his tongue between her teeth with skilful deliberation.

'This is going to be worth the wait,' he promised huskily.

'I know!' she cried blissfully. Then, 'Will you show me...?' Her eyes slid down his body and she swallowed. 'How to touch...?'

'I will,' he promised thickly.

Soon he was begging her, begging her to stop. Kat complied with the utmost reluctance, consumed by a relentless curiosity about his body. He kissed her a lot more then, and stroked and caressed her until her skin was singing.

She half closed her eyes when he slid her dress down over her hips. Her thighs trembled as she felt the garment slide lower. She could feel his eyes, through her closed eyelids, watching her. Did he like what he was seeing...? She wasn't normally plagued by insecurities about her body but, God she hoped so!

Kat's body jerked and her eyes shot open at the touch of his lips against the soft feminine curve of her belly. Her head fell back and she moaned and squirmed as his tongue continued to inscribe delicate shapes over her smooth flawless skin. All the time his hands were moving, stroking gently, skimming lower and lower.

It felt the most natural thing in the world to open her legs wide for him, invite his touch to grow more intimate. When she felt the lash of his tongue her body bucked and she cried out in protest.

Matt wouldn't let her twist away; he held her down gently but firmly while he told her in that sinfully sexy voice of his how beautiful she was, how much he needed to touch and taste her. It wasn't long before Kat's cries were of encouragement, not protest.

Kat hadn't known her body was capable of feeling this way; it reached the point where his lightest touch was driving her insane. The tiny ripples were running visibly across her stomach by the time he positioned himself between her legs.

Matt was breathing hard, his face a rigid mask of restraint. Her fingers dug in his back and she screamed shamelessly at him when he hesitated.

'I need you inside me nooow…!' she wailed, pressing desperate kisses on the smooth, hot skin of his chest.

There wasn't the pain she'd been expecting, just a deep glorious feeling of completion as she closed tightly around him. Then he was moving, stroking her inside, and she realised there was more, and more of him too, as he sank deeper into her.

Her teeth closed around his earlobe. 'I won't break,' she promised, sensing the restraint in him and wanting to break it.

It did break, and all heaven broke loose.

Lying in the curve of his arm a little later, she sighed and opened one eye.

'You were right. It was worth the wait.'

CHAPTER EIGHT

KAT saw the envelope and put down the loaded tea tray she'd been about to take back to the kitchen. Fortunately the strain that had developed between herself and the rest of the staff once it had become obvious her relationship with Matt had strayed beyond the professional—a situation that Matt was inclined to flaunt, not disguise—had started to thaw.

Perching on the arm of a chair, she opened the envelope with her name emblazoned in Matt's bold semi-illegible scrawl across the front, and peered into it curiously. Had Matt been watching, he'd have seen the colour fade dramatically from her cheeks.

There was a tremor in her fingers as she turned it upside down. The fat wad of notes fluttered out; a faint breeze from the open French doors sent them swirling across the room. 'What's this?'

Matt didn't lift his eyes from the report he was skimming through. 'Damned idiots...' he muttered. 'What was that?' he added vaguely. Fleetingly, his glance flickered over her still figure. 'Oh, it's your salary,' he announced negligently.

As he watched she lifted one pretty foot and deliberately ground a note of large denomination into the carpet. He repressed a groan as she levelled her belligerent eyes at his face. He set the report aside.

Matt Devlin didn't put work aside for women, he didn't consider he was particularly ruthless or selfish, it just wasn't him. The women he dated knew what his priorities were, if they didn't like it they didn't have to stick around.

Kat remained oblivious to the significance of his action but Matt didn't, it was just another symptom in a long line of similar glaringly obvious shifts in his attitude over the past days. He had been aware all week that his feelings for Kathleen went beyond anything he'd ever experienced before. The sex was great of course—the best—but it was way more than that…his eyes softened as they swept over her angry figure. It was hard to imagine his life without her around.

He picked up a note that had fallen onto the arm of a chintzy chair. 'What's wrong, did I miscalculate?'

She flinched as though he'd struck her and, chin held high, drew herself up to her full height, which was still a good ten inches short of his. She still managed to give the impression she was looking down at him from a great height.

Kathleen had a remarkably expressive face. He'd got pretty good at reading her expression, it often gave him pleasure to do so.

A freeze frame image of her face flashed before his eyes. Her skin was glistening damp, her eyes were closed, her lips slightly parted, she was crying his name, it was a wild, abandoned, exultant sound.

The image was so strong that his body responded lustfully to the stimulus and for a moment he was back in the privacy of the bedroom.

It was reluctantly that he released the memory and faced up to the less pleasurable present. The expression on her face at that moment wasn't one of the most enjoyable to translate; it came out as something close to, You low, loathsome worm! Even if something had been lost in translation, this definitely wasn't the sort of look to warm a man on a cold night!

'How dare you?' she breathed wrathfully.

'This is about the money…right…?'

His laconic drawl whipped her wrath and mortification to even greater heights. She stepped forward, snatched the note from his fingers and ripped it up to confetti size before she flung it in his face. How could anyone be so insensitive?

'There!' she cried, wiping a tear of anger and disillusionment from her face. 'That's what I think of you and your money. Are you *trying* to insult me?' she wondered querulously. 'What's perfectly obvious is you have no respect for me whatever.'

He shook his glossy dark head and wondered whether he'd walked into this conversation somewhere in the middle.

'I know I'm being stupid and slow, but could you explain what I've done to make you so mad?'

'*You paid me!*' she wailed.

'You work; you get paid. That's fairly normal working practice.'

'Don't patronise me!'

'For God's sake, woman, will you stop the magical mystery tour and just tell me what the problem is?'

'Leaving aside the fact I'm not due to be paid until the end of the month, the problem,' she drawled, allowing her embittered gaze to sweep disparagingly over his tall, impossibly attractive figure, 'is I'm a bit unsure as to which part of my duties you're paying me for?'

He finally realised what she was driving at. Matt's patience and understanding went up in a puff of smoke—you could almost hear the crackle as the flame caught hold—and even in the midst of her disillusioned anger Kat couldn't help but appreciate he looked pretty damned spectacular when he lost it.

'Just what exactly are you saying?' The look he shot her was pure menace.

Kat wasn't in the mood to be intimidated; she was in the mood for a fight. She'd been fool enough to think their relationship had begun to mean more to him than a shallow sexual liaison. He didn't speak of love, but his actions were loving—or was she seeing things that weren't there because she wanted to? No! They didn't just make love, they talked, sometimes late into the night; they talked of everything under the sun, and Kat remembered every precious syllable. Now he'd spoilt it all with some cheap trick like this.

'I'm wondering what sort of man sleeps with a woman and then pays her money. Hell!' Her scornful laughter rang out liltingly. 'I'm surprised you didn't leave it on the pillow! Isn't that the usual form?' At this point, she noticed in an objective sort of way that he looked murderously furious. 'I'll have you know I'm not a commodity to be bought and sold as and when it suits you.' With a scornful gesture she turned her back on him.

He caught her upper arm and swung her around.

'My God,' he rasped, 'you don't rate yourself very highly—or, for that matter, me!'

'Let me go!' Kat felt the tears begin to trickle slowly down her face. Rather than let him see them, see how much he'd hurt her, she kept her pink-tipped nose pointed at the floor.

'Look at me, Kathleen.'

Matt cupped his hand around her chin when it became perfectly obvious she was going to do nothing of the sort. His self-righteous anger couldn't withstand the abject misery on her tear-stained face; all of a sudden all he wanted to do was kiss her tremulous lips.

'If I'm guilty of anything, angel,' he said throatily, 'it's of not thinking. And if you're guilty of anything...'

Despite everything Kat's lips quivered in amusement. 'Have you ever in your life made an apology without qualifying it?'

He had the grace to look sheepish. 'Listen, I know your salary was supposed to be paid into your bank account at the end of the month, but I've been getting the impression your mysterious financial problems—'

'They're not mysterious!' It wasn't until she heard the defensive sharpness in her voice that Kat realised how deeply ingrained the habit of playing down her money problems had actually become.

She'd not consciously withheld the information, but she did feel very protective of her mother's memory; it seemed disloyal to go bad-mouthing her when she wasn't here to defend herself.

'I'm not fishing for information,' he responded in a soothing manner.

Of course, it would be nice if she felt she could confide in him! That she trusted him enough. It was getting hard to ignore the fact that every time an opportunity arose for her to explain she neatly side-stepped the issue.

'I just got the idea that things were urgent.'

Matt wasn't used to being around women who stubbornly insisted on paying their way; what had started out seeming charming and sweet was fast becoming irritating. It was hard not to feel insulted, especially when she threw a gift he'd taken a lot of care choosing back in his face!

'Very nice. But I couldn't possibly...' Had been her starchy response when he'd presented her with a string of antique pearls.

'I don't like to see you looking worried.'

The sincerity the gruffness of his explanation couldn't disguise affected Kat more deeply than a thousand flowery sentiments.

'Oh! That's...lovely.' She felt the last dregs of her animosity disintegrate.

'Life's going to be a lot simpler around here if we keep our personal and professional lives separate...'

Kat stopped mid-sniff, her eyes widening with incredulity; she was constantly amazed by Matt's ability to reconstruct events to suit his purposes.

'Separate? Like when I was trying to give you your massage yesterday?' she enquired innocently.

A few hours each day spent outdoors and Matt's pallor had been replaced by the beginnings of healthy-looking tan.

That glow grew a little deeper now, under her quizzical stare. A slash of colour appeared across the crest of his cheekbones.

'That was different.'

Kat turned her head until her cheek rested in the palm of his hand; she was willing to let this palpable untruth go unchallenged. The hurt was beginning to fade; she knew she'd reacted so dramatically because she felt insecure about their relationship. Things had happened so quickly... She'd got in so deep, yet for all she knew it could all be over tomorrow.

'I don't work for you, Matt.'

The thumb which had been stroking the soft angle of her jawline stilled. 'You mean you're quitting on me? Because of this?' Both hands slid to her waist and he jerked her roughly towards him.

'I mean that as far as I'm concerned I haven't been working for you since we became lovers!' Her eyes were openly loving as they scanned his face. 'I couldn't do both, you see, and when it came to making a choice there was no competition. I'm already looking for another job.'

'The hell you are!' he exclaimed, looking totally gobsmacked by her matter-of-fact announcement.

'Well, you're not going to need me much longer.'

Kat was so busy being stoical in defiance of the wave of misery that washed over at the thought of Matt not needing her that she didn't see the shocked expression in Matt's blue eyes.

Sometimes a man couldn't see what had been staring him in the face all along.

'Is that so...?'

'Well, no,' she replied, puzzled by his aggressive tone. 'You're so much better, and you said yourself that you won't be staying here much longer. They're advertising for a replacement at my old hospital, a temporary job to fill in for maternity leave...'

'You don't need a job,' he announced abruptly.

'I do!' And the sooner, the better. This seemed as good a time as any to explain about her mother's financial mess. 'As you already know, I've got debts...'

His broad shoulders lifted dismissively. 'I'll sort those,' he said abruptly.

She stiffened. 'You mean you'll pay them...?'

'Come and live with me when I move out of here.'

To a stunned Kat he sounded incredibly off-hand and unemotional about it. 'Just like that?' she echoed, feeling her temper steadily rising.

'It's not complicated.'

Kat gave a squeal of pure fury. His grip remained stubbornly firm as she wriggled furiously to free herself. She gave up and instead pinned him with a blank stare. Her eyes were as hot as her expression was cold.

'You think I'd give up my independence, my freedom, my self-respect?' Her voice rose to a scornful crescendo. 'All at a nod from you? You just don't listen, do you, Matt? I don't want to be a kept woman!'

'Fine, then marry me.' It emerged in an off-hand, if-you've-got-nothing-better-to-do, why-not? sort of way—she'd probably laugh in his face, he decided, closing his eyes.

The problem was, Matt had no experience to draw upon in this area; he'd had zero practice proposing. He'd never even contemplated doing so until a few moments ago—to be precise the moment she had said he didn't need her any more. It was then he'd accepted what had been staring him in the face all along, that not only did he need this woman, he needed her in the for ever after sense!

The air whooshed out of Kat's lungs in one protracted gasp.

'*What did you say?*'

'Marry me.'

Dazed, Kat gazed up into his darkly fringed eyes; they were fierce and compelling.

'You can work if you want. You can do what you like. But marry me.'

'Why?'

Kat held her breath; it had taken all her self-control not to grab him and scream, *Yes!*

'Why?' she asked again, boldly.

Please, please, *please* let him say he loves me. Kat couldn't think of another logical reason why he would propose. She hadn't exactly been playing hard to get; it wasn't as if he had to marry her to get her into bed. Which sort of left an unbelievable option—he wanted more than that from her!

His lips had actually parted when the door burst open. Kat could have wept with sheer frustration.

To say her expression was unfriendly as she turned towards the door would have been a massive understatement. The expression on Matt's face was even less welcoming.

Neither of these facts seemed to make any impression on their visitor.

'Mother!' Matt regarded his elegant parent with a heavy scowl. 'What are you doing here?'

'The last I heard, this is my house,' Drusilla pointed out tartly.

The older woman's eyes swept around the room but they passed over Kat unseeingly. Kat hardly registered the vague expression in her blue eyes; it was taking all her time to cope with the aftermath of anticlimax.

She shot a covert glance at Matt's profile from under the sweep of her lashes and saw he was looking right back at her. There was nothing ambiguous about the devastatingly direct stare; it was hot and hungry. Her tummy muscles started twanging like overstretched guitar strings.

'I'm here because...'

Like a sleepwalker, Kat tore her eyes from Matt's face

with difficulty and saw the extraordinary spectacle of Drusilla's face crumbling. She seemed to shrink somehow before Kat's horrified eyes.

'I've left your father!' she wailed as tears began to ooze from beneath her delicately tinted eyelids. With a loud sob she flung herself into her son's arms.

The action took Matt unawares. Neither of his parents had ever been demonstrative in a tactile way. His rewards had not taken the form of hugs and kisses.

The awkward way he patted his mother's back made Kat's tender heart squeeze in her chest. From the expression on his face, it looked as if she wasn't the only one who was wishing she was elsewhere! There had been a tinge of desperate appeal in the look he'd sent her over his mother's head.

She smiled encouragingly as he mouthed 'sorry' over Drusilla's head. Kat was content to luxuriate in the warm promise of his smile... He'd proposed... He wanted to marry her! It seemed selfish to feel so deliriously happy while Drusilla was suffering so much, but she couldn't help it; if she got any happier she might just explode!

When presently Drusilla lifted her head from her son's shoulder there were mascara stains all over his blue chambray shirt.

'Sorry,' she sniffed, raising a delicate lacy hanky to her nose.

'What's he done?' Matt's grim expression boded ill for his absent parent.

'He's the most stubborn, aggravating, *unnatural* man in the world!' came the dramatic throbbing reply.

Matt relaxed. He'd been steeling himself for something a lot juicier, a youthful mistress at the very least—although, to be fair, Connor Devlin's numerous faults did not to his knowledge include a wandering eye. If they had, Matt would have confronted him a long time ago!

Irritation was mingled with his relief. His mother had

taken thirty plus years to figure out what a bastard she was married to...couldn't she have waited a few minutes longer to share the news with him?

Before he replied to his mother's announcement, his restless gaze flickered towards Kathleen, who was stealthily sidling towards the door with a furtive expression on her face.

'So what's new? He's been all those things for the past thirty years and that's never bothered you before.'

'You've no idea how I've suffered.'

Her expression grew irritated as her only son remained palpably unimpressed by her tragic tale.

'Perhaps I should leave,' Kat said quietly as she took up a strategic position bedside the door.

'Stay where you are!' Matt blasted without even turning to look at her.

His peremptory tone froze her to the spot for a few seconds. Pretty quickly the shock began to wear off and her truculent expression made it pretty clear she'd taken serious umbrage at his dictatorial command. She was just about to tell him in no uncertain terms where he could stick his orders when he entreated in a softer, harassed-sounding tone, *'Please.'*

What girl could resist an appeal like that from a big hunky man she was blindly in love with?—not Kat! In her soft and mushy condition she wouldn't have refused him anything.

'Kathleen, my dear, how are you?' Kat marvelled that even in the midst of calamity Drusilla still had beautifully polished manners.

On cloud nine, embarrassed to hell—take your choice. Either way she didn't think the distracted Drusilla would notice what she said.

Kat smiled uneasily. 'I'll go and organise some tea, shall I?' Tea had a comforting sound about it. Even though Kat herself was a coffee drinker, she could sup with the best of them in times of stress. If in doubt, drink tea, make tea or talk about the weather—it was the British answer to therapy, and much cheaper.

'How kind...'

'Stay put!'

Drusilla threw her son an exasperated look. 'Can't you see the girl is embarrassed?'

'That's as maybe, but it's best if she knows what sort of family she's marrying into.'

'I didn't say yes,' Kat disclaimed weakly.

'*Yet!*' Matt cut in grimly.

His arrogant certainty should have appalled her. So what did she do? Read him the riot act...condemn his rampant display of chauvinism...? No, she just stared up at him with her heart in her eyes and her bosom heaving with foolish, breathless excitement!

There was a bemused expression on Drusilla's face as she looked from one young person to the other. Her first instinct had been to assume this was all some bizarre joke—she never had been able to understand her only child's sense of humour. Then she saw that look in Matt's eyes—she hadn't known Matthew was capable of looking like that—as they rested on Kat's flushed face. The expression in the girl's eyes was nothing short of blind adoration!

An expression of wonder drifted across her face.

'When I set...' Drusilla blushed guiltily. 'I n-never expected...'

'You finally struck gold, Mother, as did I.' Matt interrupted his parent's stuttering incredulity with barely concealed impatience.

It took Kat a few seconds to decipher the back-handed compliment; when she did she began to glow with pleasure.

'I'm still not quite clear why you've left my father.'

The vaguest hint of criticism in her son's voice brought a frown to Drusilla's smooth brow. 'You left.'

'I'm not married to him.'

'Neither will I be, soon,' she announced in faltering accents; then, a lot more stoutly, 'I'd have thought you of all people would understand. He's gone too far this time, throwing his orders about, expecting me to jump...' She brooded darkly.

Kat found this description uncannily familiar; being a tactful girl, she didn't mention the family resemblance.

'It's you I'm concerned about! Do you know he's disinherited you—*you*, his only son!' she exclaimed.

'Has he only just got around to that? I thought he'd done it years ago,' Matt interjected. His expression suggested mild surprise rather than horror.

'He's got this silly idea of leaving everything to some sort of charitable trust! The Connor Devlin Foundation,' she sneered. 'I think it's his way of buying immortality. And, to make it worse, he wants me to do the same! I told him—' She stopped abruptly and directed a startled gaze in her son's direction. 'You *knew?* And you don't care? Matthew, it's your birthright!'

Matt shrugged. 'It's money,' he corrected drily. 'Dad doesn't owe me anything.'

From her perplexed expression it was clear Drusilla couldn't begin to comprehend her son's vexing attitude.

'Well, you're having my money, including this place, no matter what you or your father say!' she threatened sternly. 'It was the final straw when he had the gall to tell me I should choose between him and my own son. One ultimatum too far! Well, I did choose!' she announced with a triumphant grin which morphed into a wobbly miserable sob.

'Good God, mother!' Matt exclaimed in an exasperated accent. 'You know he doesn't mean half the things he says when he's in a rage. Why didn't you just wait for him to cool down?'

Drusilla's damp eyelids lifted. 'Like *you* did?'

Kat watched as Matt's lean body tensed, as his strong features grew taunt and remote.

'That wasn't the same thing at all,' he replied with daunting formality.

Drusilla threw up her hands in despair.

'It wouldn't be, would it?' She turned to Kat. 'I hope you know what you're letting yourself in for, marrying a Devlin man.' Her angry attention switched back to her son. 'I sometimes think you and your father enjoy your little feud!' she accused resentfully. 'And while you're both busy waging war, who is it left trying to please you both? *Me!* Well, I've had enough!' She collapsed gracefully into a button-backed nursing chair.

'Now look what you've done!' Kat reproached crossly, dropping on her knees beside the weeping woman.

'Women!' Matt snarled, crossing to the drinks cabinet. He selected a brandy and filled the bottom of a balloon.

'I don't like brandy,' his mother reminded him.

'It's not for you,' her unfeeling son announced, emptying the contents in one swallow.

There were the unmistakable sounds of a disturbance in the hallway. Kat could hear the deep growl of an angry male voice.

'Oh, God!' Drusilla moaned in a doom laden tone. 'It's your father!'

Under Kat's startled gaze, she leapt up, glanced at herself critically in the mirror over the mantel and, once satisfied all was as it ought to be, arranged herself gracefully in the chair once more.

One thing was obvious—Drusilla was delighted her husband had followed her.

Even without Drusilla's warning, Kat couldn't have mistaken the identity of the man who strode into the room. There was no dramatic likeness, though the firm uncompromising line of his jaw and the sweep of his broad brow were identical to Matt's. The similarities were cumulative,

and had more to do with little things like the way he held
his head, the familiar frown.

He was almost as tall as his son, but whereas Matt's lean
athletic frame would grow sparer with the passing years
this man's build was more thickset and bullish, but he
looked comfortable carrying the extra pounds. A big man
in an expensive suit who oozed authority.

His authority faltered for a split second when he saw the
tall figure calmly watching him—he recovered fast.

For Matt's sake, Kat was prepared to dislike him on
sight.

'I might have known *you'd* be behind all this,' the older
man jeered. 'You've been poisoning her mind against me
for years!'

Matt moved to place himself between his father and the
two women, whom so far the older man had totally ignored.
Connor Devlin's stride was so close to a blatant swagger
that had the situation been less tense Kat might have
laughed. The testosterone levels in the room were probably
illegal, she reflected ruefully, but, failing government
guidelines on the subject, they were definitely uncomfortable. *Extremely* uncomfortable!

'I'm here to talk to your mother, not you.'

Matt folded his arms across his chest; his position effectively cut Drusilla off from view. 'Talk away.'

Connor Devlin's ruddy colour deepened. *'Alone!'* he bellowed.

Matt's lips curled scornfully. 'I get the impression that
Mother doesn't want to talk to you, alone or otherwise,' he
announced in a slow, provocative drawl.

One glance at the pained expression on Drusilla's face
told Kat that nothing could have been further from the truth.
She could stand back and let this macho stand-off degenerate into a mud-slinging match or worse, or she could do
something about it. Cold water might work, but as there

wasn't any to hand she'd have to think of something a bit more subtle.

She bent forward and whispered quietly in Drusilla's ear. The older woman looked startled; after a moment, she nodded. Kat smiled and stepped forward.

'Actually,' she said in clear voice, 'Drusilla would be grateful if you left the room for a moment…both of you,' she added with more assurance than she was feeling.

The big men paused in the midst of their macho posturing to glare at her.

Kat's eyes skimmed past the older man. Matt saw the challenge in her droll smile and the fire slowly faded from his eyes. He began to look thoughtful. What was she up to…?

'And who might you be?' Connor Devlin demanded.

'Your future daughter-in-law.' Matt's azure eyes burnt into hers with an intimate mixture of humour and exasperated pride.

'That remains to be seen,' she countered silkily.

Matt grinned, but there was something satisfyingly determined about the sexy curve of his lips… Mind you, where Matt's lips were concerned she wasn't exactly objective.

'Since when have you been engaged?' Matt's estranged father demanded indignantly. 'You didn't say a word, Drusilla!' he barked.

'I thought I wasn't meant to mention Matthew's name in your presence, Connor…?'

Connor Devlin cleared his throat and looked badtempered at the reminder. 'It's never stopped you before.'

'Come on, Father,' Matt said touching his father lightly on the shoulder.

The contact made the older man stiffen, but Kat noticed that was as far as his protest went.

'Come and have a look at the rose garden.'

'*My* rose garden,' Connor added pointedly.

'Actually, dear,' Drusilla piped in sweetly, 'it's mine.'

Her husband looked ready to explode as Matt led him from the room. 'What's wrong with your own place?' they heard him demand as he left the room.

'Too many stairs.'

'Stairs, my foot! Freeloading off me...!'

'That man!' his wife exclaimed, looking mortified. 'He didn't leave the hospital until Matt was off the critical list, you know, but he forbade me to tell him he'd been there. What can I do?'

'Well, ignore what he says for a start,' Kat said. She could see that the idea shocked Drusilla. 'Think about it,' she advised. 'He said you had to choose between him and Matt—you did, and what did he do...? He followed you. Don't you see, the man clearly adores you? I think it's about time you started throwing around some ultimatums of your own.'

They caught up with the menfolk about half an hour later in the rose garden; they weren't talking horticulture.

'It was a criminally reckless thing to do!'

'Going soft in your old age, Dad...?'

'You cocky young pup!'

'Connor, enough!'

Connor Devlin was clearly startled by his wife's tone.

'Don't say another word until I've finished. I've put up with this nonsense for years. I refuse to spend another Christmas without my son—' her affectionate glance travelled towards Kat '—and his wife, and before long—who knows?—my grandchildren.

'All this,' she continued in a disgusted tone, 'just because he didn't do what you wanted, Connor. The fact is you're as proud as Punch of what he's achieved.' She ignored the inarticulate protest that gurgled in her husband's throat 'And don't you look so smug, Matthew. You're just as stiff-

necked and inflexible as he is. Either you two shake hands
and make up or I've done with the pair of you.'

'And I won't marry you if your father's not at the wedding,' Kat added by way of an extra inducement. She hoped
nobody would notice she had her fingers firmly crossed.
Flood and fire wouldn't keep her from marrying Matt!

She could tell by the way Matt was looking at her that
he knew she was lying her head off. She hoped he wouldn't
call her bluff in front of everyone, especially after she'd
won over Drusilla with her 'sisters must be strong' act.

'In that case,' Matt said, his eyes firmly fixed upon hers,
'consider yourself invited.' He turned to his father and extended his hand and looked his father directly in the eye.

Kat held her breath. She was pretty sure she wasn't the
only one. Just when she thought she'd miscalculated,
Connor Devlin thrust his hand out to his son.

It would be too much to say that everything got cosy,
even though much laughter and tears followed, but Kat was
satisfied that things were moving in the right direction.

Later, when they were finally alone, Matt planted his
hands on the wall beside her head and leaned towards her.
It was more a promise than a threat.

'Well, you little witch, are you pleased with yourself?'

Kat's eyes sparkled back up at him. 'I don't know what
you're talking about,' she replied, tongue firmly tucked in
her cheek.

Matt threw back his dark head and laughed. 'Sure you
don't. I suppose you think you've got all the Devlins eating
out of your little hand now...' He lifted her hand and
pressed his open mouth to her palm. Kat sighed as delicious
little quivers ran all the way up her arm.

Her eyes darkened dramatically. 'I only want one Devlin
to eat out of my hand,' she insisted huskily.

Matt looked at the invitation glowing in her eyes and he
inhaled sharply. 'You haven't given me your answer yet.'

Kat traced the outline of her lips with the tip of her

tongue. She felt the shudder that ran all the way through his tall loose-limbed frame.

'Remind me what the question was,' she whispered huskily.

His nostrils flared as his eyes ran hungrily over her flushed face. 'Marry me?' he purred.

Kat grinned cheekily and ducked under his arm. She skipped backwards across the room. Matt had been running away from those in hot matrimonial pursuit for so long, perhaps it wouldn't do him any harm to do the running himself for once...not that Kat had any intention of running too far or too hard!

'Maybe,' she carolled sweetly—just before she tripped over a stray shoe she'd kicked off a little earlier.

She landed on her bottom with an undignified bump; before she had time to see if he was laughing at her plight, she felt herself being hauled to her feet. The hands curled around her upper arms clamped her arms to her sides and brought her up onto her tiptoes. She could feel the hard strength of him; the warm male scent of him made her nostrils quiver.

'*Maybe...?*' he prompted grimly. The tense, driven expression on his face suggested this wasn't a subject Matt took lightly.

'A definite maybe...?' Her sultry smile faltered and faded totally beneath the driving intensity of his hard tense scrutiny. 'Yes!' she cried urgently. 'Yes, please, I will marry you, Matt...' Her eyes brimmed; her throat clogged with emotion.

Triumph blazed to life in his eyes. He brought his face down close to hers. Kat couldn't blink, she couldn't breathe.

'Why will you marry me, my little witch?'

'Because I love you, Matt, deeply, madly, *desperately!*' she cried.

The intensity of her declaration seemed to take him

aback for a moment. Dark colour ran up under his skin as he stared down at her with a stunned, un-Matt-like expression. She saw the muscles of his throat work.

'Thank God for that,' he breathed, just before his dark head bent forward. Kat's lips parted eagerly under the insistent pressure of his marauding lips.

'I can't stand up,' she complained weakly when he'd eventually had his fill.

'Now you know how I felt.'

The memory of his suffering brought a cloud to her sunny horizon. 'Don't joke about it...' she began fiercely. 'What are you doing?' she gasped as he swept her off her feet.

'Loving you. Do you mind?'

Kat curved her arms tightly around his neck as he lifted her across the bed. 'Not in the least,' she admitted happily.

I have everything I could ever want, she thought dreamily as his lips touched her neck, her throat, her lips... This is the start of my very own happy-ever-after. Nothing can spoil it.

Or so she thought!

CHAPTER NINE

His mother leaned through the car window once more and caught hold of the loose hem of Matt's shirt; she tugged him down to eye level.

'How many more times are you going to say goodbye, woman?' her husband enquired wearily. 'I lost count at around five.' He didn't act as if he expected his wife to pay any heed to him.

'The moment I saw her I knew she was right for you.' Drusilla's eyes filled with tears. 'I just didn't know if you'd be bright enough to realise it too. I'm so glad you are. Now everything's turned out perfectly. I know Amy was desperately worried about how the poor girl would cope with those wretched gambling debts once she was gone,' she confided. 'Amy wouldn't tell me how bad they were,' she chattered on, oblivious to the frozen expression on her son's face. 'Which makes me suspect they were pretty bad.' She looked to Matt for confirmation of her suspicions.

'Pretty bad,' he agreed, straightening up. He banged on the roof of the car, causing his father to protest vigorously from inside. Matt responded mechanically to a fresh outbreak of a final round of goodbyes.

Kat stood in the doorway, the stone flags cold under her bare feet, and waited for Matt to turn around and join her. When he didn't, she felt puzzled; when the seconds became minutes and the minutes multiplied, she felt seriously concerned. He hadn't moved an inch since the car carrying his parents had pulled away.

She called his name a couple of times but the wind must have snatched it away because still he didn't move. Worriedly, she went back indoors to search out a pair of shoes.

She shoved her feet into the first pair she came across—which happened to be an old pair of Matt's tennis shoes. Kat wasn't much bothered what sort of fashion statement she was making.

'Matt...?' Warily she touched his arm, her fingers closing over compact muscle. As always when she touched him, she was aware of the steely hardness in his body, the promise of strength. It was the first time she'd ever touched him and sensed rejection. With a tiny gasp of dismay she stepped back, her eyes wide and confused.

She gave her head a tiny shake, inclined to write off her initial impression to an over-active imagination, but the chill around her heart still didn't disperse. Then he turned to face her and she knew she'd not been imagining anything. His face would have held more warmth had it been carved of stone.

'What's wrong, Matt...?'

Bad—it had to be something bad to make him look like that. She sought around wildly for a probable cause for that awful empty look in his eyes. Had he and his father had words again...?

'Is it true that your financial problems are gambling debts?'

Kat's eyes widened. It was the last thing she had expected to hear. Was that all...? If anything, she felt relieved. He was probably a bit narked that she hadn't confided in him yet...

'Did Drusilla tell you? I meant to explain,' she told him frankly, 'but to be honest it was a bit embarrassing.'

'I can imagine.'

The pucker between her brows deepened. He sounded really strange, and he was still radiating that *hands off* thing that made her feel afraid to touch him. Her tummy muscles cramped with panic.

'Now you know all my secrets,' she babbled brightly.

Her attempt at levity fell flat on its face. Something was going on here she didn't understand.

'Until the next time,' he responded heavily.

'Pardon...?' The pain in his eyes just didn't make any sense.

'There's always a next time with compulsive gamblers. You could say,' he explained, with a self-derisive laugh, 'that I have had some experience of how deceitful and plausible they can be...'

'Good God!' she gasped. 'You think *I*...' Her expression cleared she caught hold of his arm. 'You don't understand!' she cried.

'Oh, but I do!' he grated grimly. 'Maybe that's the problem. I know it's a disease, and you need help...therapy. I want to help, but I've got to be brutally honest here, Kathleen I'm not sure I can. I've been standing here thinking about it, and I still don't know.' His clouded blue eyes looked dully into the distance. 'It's all about trust, and the bottom line is I don't know if I'll ever be able to trust you. There'll always be a nagging doubt at the back of my mind...'

The explanation that would have solved everything withered on her tongue. *Trust.* She bit back the hysterical urge to laugh...or was it cry...? He was right, this was all about trust. Kat felt as if she were encased in ice. Her hand fell from his arm and she pressed her fingers against the throbbing points of pain at her temples.

'So what you're actually saying is that if I'm a compulsive gambler you don't want anything to do with me?'

'*If!* You see—you're denying you've got a problem.'

'From where I'm standing, the only problem I've got is you!' she yelled back bitterly.

'I'm not turning my back on you, Kathleen. I couldn't, even if I wanted to...'

'Then you want to?'

'Maybe I do have a problem,' he admitted, brushing his

hand through his thick glossy hair in a gesture that was intensely weary. 'But so do you.' His disillusioned sombre eyes avoided her face like a man avoiding a hot fire. 'I'm just being honest with you, telling you how I feel. I've got a history, you see, of...'

'Oh, you told me about the partner who nearly gambled away your precious company. And they say lightning doesn't strike in the same place twice!' she sneered, and a flicker of anger crossed his face. 'Well, you needn't worry. It will be quite safe from me—because I wouldn't marry a man whose idea of for better or worse is to bale out the instant things get rough. I just consider myself lucky that I found that out before things got complicated.' God, yes, she felt *very* lucky...lucky as in winning the lottery and losing the ticket!

'You don't call this complicated?'

Kat gave a careless shrug. 'Like you said, we didn't have a contract, and as far as I'm concerned we just terminated our arrangement. I mean, I wouldn't want to be around the next time you lost a fiver out of your wallet... And I believe these are yours, too.' She slipped out of the well-worn tennis shoes and shoved them at him.

'Don't be stupid! We can make this right...'

For a moment her protective shield of anger slipped... How she wanted to believe him...how she wanted things to go back to the way they'd been. She lifted her pain-filled grey eyes to his.

'Do you actually believe that, Matt? Or is it just wishful thinking?' she whispered. She saw the tell-tale flicker of doubt in those deep blue depths and with a brittle laugh she rushed on.

'And this is yours too.' She tugged off the snug-fitting engagement ring, an antique that had belonged to his grandmother—Matt had called it fate when it had fitted her like a glove. She held it out to him. 'I was going to pawn it tomorrow, but what the hell? Easy come, easy go—you know how it is with us high rollers!'

'Kathleen!' He flung the shoes and ring aside and plunged after the bare-footed figure fleeing up the driveway. The gravel must have been tearing her feet to shreds but she didn't seem to notice. He caught up with her and without saying a word scooped her up and carried her over the rest of the uneven surface.

The last time, she thought as she was carried along by those strong arms. The last time this will happen. The last time a lot of things would happen. The sense of loss that permeated her entire being was akin to bereavement.

Kat's chest was heaving with a combination of physical exertion and emotional turmoil by the time he placed her back on her feet.

'Don't leave me.'

It couldn't be a plea. Matt Devlin didn't beg... Her eyes flickered to his face. The only information she gleaned was that he was the most incredibly attractive man she'd ever seen—and she'd already known that. His expression was frustratingly unrevealing.

'Why?' She gave him the chance to come up with something really good, and it looked as if he was going to come up with the goods. He looked like a man fighting a particularly vicious internal battle and getting nowhere fast... Kat withdrew her gaze hastily. She couldn't afford to get empathic; she had her own problems—problems such as her heart was breaking.

'You love me...?' she suggested, making it sound like a joke.

She watched his mouth harden.

'I thought not. You've never said it before, so why start now when it's so obviously not true?'

Before, she'd been so deliriously happy she'd been prepared to overlook the fact he'd never once told her he loved her, even though she'd babbled on about her own love *ad nauseum*…actions speak louder than words, she'd told herself. Now she knew differently; now she knew he'd never said it because he didn't!

'Love has nothing to do with this, Kathleen. You need help.'

'I need a taxi,' she contradicted, mounting the stairs.

'I'll help you through this…'

'Because you're that sort of guy,' she mocked. 'Thanks, but no thanks, Matt. To be frank, it makes me sick to look at you!' she told him coldly.

She didn't look back to see what effect her words had had on him, but he didn't follow her—that said it all.

'I thought I was being paranoid at first. Then I checked for obvious things, like was my skirt tucked in my knickers, or…?'

'God, yes, do you remember when Mrs Rutherford at—?'

'Don't change the subject, Andie,' Kat cut in impatiently. 'Why is half the hospital staring at me as if I've got two heads? Why are people muttering behind their hands and why do conversations stop dead when I walk into a room?' she finished hotly.

With a sigh, Andie thrust her hand deep into her capacious shoulder bag. She extracted a dog-eared magazine and, avoiding Kat's eyes passed it to her.

'I didn't believe it…honestly…'

The well-thumbed magazine fell open at the relevant double-page spread.

'Up To His Old Tricks!!' the main headline shrieked. The one under the half-page colour picture was only slightly less prominent. 'This isn't available on the NHS,' was the witty caption under a large glossy photo of herself sitting astride a bare-chested Matt. Her shirt was open to the waist, revealing a lacy bra.

Kat could recall the occasion when they'd been sitting

beside the lake in the grounds. It had started off innocently enough; she'd been massaging his shoulders, then he'd turned over and... The way she recalled it, if it hadn't started raining at that point the photo could have been a lot worse!

Kat's knuckles turned whiter than the paper she gripped as her eyes, which seemed to be the only part of her that could move at that moment, skimmed over the item.

Millionaire Matt Devlin recuperating at a country retreat with the help of his private physiotherapist, Miss Kathleen Wray.

She read on. It didn't come right out and say that she was being paid for her expertise in the bedroom but it might just as well have!

'Oh, my God!' she groaned. 'Everyone has seen this and...I think I'm going to be sick...' She pressed her hands to her abdomen and rocked forward.

'Take some deep breaths,' an anxious Andie advised, draping her arm over the younger girl's shoulders. 'That's it...good girl. It could be worse.'

Kat looked at her friend as if she'd gone mad.

'I'd kill for a body like yours,' her friend admitted frankly. 'Call me twisted, but the idea of every red-blooded male under ninety lusting after...'

Her friend's well-meaning comfort was having quite the opposite effect on Kat, who visibly cringed at the prospect of male eyes following her, thinking...*ugh!*

'I don't want to be lusted after!' Kat wailed.

'Not even by *him?*' her friend wondered with an envious sigh.

'Especially not him!' Kat cried. She could see her friend was just aching to ask for details but she had no intention of obliging. Why, she wondered, does this have to happen now, when I was over him...? God! I can't even lie con-vincingly to myself, she thought bleakly.

The rest of that afternoon was nothing short of a night-mare. She tried telling herself her new-found notoriety would be soon forgotten if she kept her head down; only each fresh stare and titter made it hard to believe.

She was halfway across the car park when she was way-laid by Dr Parker, the newish young registrar who had a penchant for fast cars and, despite the quiet wife at home, pretty student nurses; Kat found him pathetic.

'Kat, just the girl I've been looking for...'

'I'm off duty,' she said, increasing her pace to avoid the arm that was zeroing in on her waist.

'What a happy coincidence. So am I. What say we do something about it...?'

Kat had no choice but to come to an abrupt halt as he moved to block her path through the narrow space between a row of cars.

Kat lifted her chin. 'I'm going home,' she said quietly. 'I suggest you do the same. The way I hear it your wife doesn't see very much of you.'

Kat decided anger gave the handsome Dr Parker all the appeal of a sulky schoolboy...less, actually.

'What's wrong, Kat? You only up for it if there's enough money involved?' he sneered in a voice pitched loud enough to be heard over half the crowded car park.

Kat flinched, but her chin went up proudly—she'd done nothing she was ashamed of.

'Move out of my way.'

The sneering medic tried to stare her down but failed.

He started to move, but was making a bit of meal of it to prolong Kat's humiliation, when a hand on the collar of his white coat literally hauled him to one side. He landed against the side of a car with a loud thump.

'What the hell?' An unpleasant look on his face, the young doctor looked up and found hell in the cold blue eyes of the big man who stood glaring down at him. It wasn't an area he felt inclined to explore further! He knew it was a physical impossibility for bone marrow to freeze, but his felt seriously chilled.

His worried eyes flickered furtively from the tall man to Kat and back again. 'Not to worry...' he remarked with nervous bonhomie as he brushed off his crumpled sleeve. 'Accidents will happen.'

'It wasn't an accident.'

Like his remark, there was no middle ground in Matt's outfit; he was dressed in monochromatic colours—black jeans, white shirt. A stunned Kat couldn't stop herself examining every tiny detail of his appearance like an addict who'd been denied her fix too long.

It was possible that it was just the outfit that made him look leaner, but there was no question mark over the meaner component; Matt was simmering with barely repressed rage. Tall, imperious, with the sort of presence you couldn't buy at any price, he made an impressive and daunting picture. He looked even more heart-stoppingly spectacular than she remembered.

'What are you doing here?'

Greg Parker gave a sigh of relief as those cold blue eyes finally left his face. The guy had never looked that *big* in the papers.

'I came to take you home.'

She didn't have to ask why today...? It was that wretched magazine article; he was probably about to accuse her of feeding the story to the scuzzy rag!

Kat sighed. *Home!* That word might have had an entirely different meaning, she thought wistfully, if he'd trusted her.

Lately she'd been wondering about the trust thing. Was it possible she'd been a little too hasty in the heat of the moment, herself? Now, as always when unwanted doubts arose to spoil her perception of the occasion, she reminded herself that she might have walked away, but he'd done the pushing.

It was always at the most inconvenient moments—like now—when objectivity of sorts kicked in and she could see how gutted Matt must have felt, after his previous bad experience, believing she was up to her ears in gambling debts. It wasn't the money; for Matt it was the subterfuge and lies, and, having experienced them first-hand herself, she could appreciate his horror. The bottom line was he'd been honest—brutally honest, true, but at least he hadn't pretended.

From the way he was looking at the sexy blonde—*How was he supposed to know they still had something going?*—Greg thought it likely nobody would notice if he slipped quietly away. He soon discovered he was wrong.

'Haven't you forgotten something?' The silky smooth voice made the younger man freeze.

'I have…?'

'I believe you want to apologise to the lady?'

'Of course, of course. No offence intended.' He turned a nervous strained smile in Kat's direction.

Plenty taken, she wanted to say, but didn't. Her shoulders lifted in an infinitesimal shrug of lofty dismissal. As he vanished, her shoulders sagged and a deep sigh was dragged from the confines of her tight chest.

'Bad day?'

The unexpected tenderness she saw in Matt's eyes brought the sting of tears to Kat's eyes.

'I've had better,' she admitted gruffly. 'How are you? You look well…' she trilled brightly.

His dark brows arched. 'Are you being deliberately facetious?' he gritted.

Kat swallowed convulsively. She was painfully conscious it must seem ridiculous that she was acting as if they were two casual acquaintances.

'No, just nervous!'

She saw Matt's eyes widen in shock. What did the man expect, just materialising like that with no warning?

'I always babble when I'm nervous.'

The direction of Matt's distracted gaze made her belatedly aware that she was chewing the end of her ponytail.

'I bite my nails in moments of extreme stress too,' she explained with a weak smile that didn't reach her wide anxious eyes.

Their eyes met and clung in a way that made Kat's tummy muscles twang. God, but she'd missed him; she hadn't realised just how much until now. His hard expression abruptly softened, making it easier to spot the fact he looked as if he'd not slept for days. Kat was shocked by the haggard cast of his handsome features.

'I look like hell, Kathleen.'

Maybe he'd read her thoughts…?

'No!' She rejected this preposterous claim without thinking.

What if the shadowy hollows beneath his high cheekbones *were* more pronounced than when she'd last seen him, and there were similar dark hollows in intriguing places all over his strong-boned face? He was still spectacularly gorgeous.

'You're…' There was an awkward pause. She could hardly tell him how beautiful he was, could she?

Unexpectedly, Matt came to her assistance.

'Tired of being gawped at?' he said, catching the eye of one unfortunate gawper and reducing her to a blushing blob.

'You get used to it.'

Matt's eyes narrowed at the bitter note in her voice. 'You shouldn't have to.'

'Why are you here, Matt?'

'I told you, I came to take you home.'

'Some of us use public transport…'

'Not tonight, unless you like to be stared at.'

Kat gulped and shook her head, her eyes reflecting the horror that had been her afternoon on public display.

He nodded his head. 'Then come with me.'

To the ends of the earth!

What, she wondered as she meekly allowed Matt to take her by the arm and lead her to an opulent-looking coupé he was driving, would he have done if she had said it out loud?

A complete dunce when it came to motors, she had no idea what make it was, but some of the admirers gathered around it obviously did. They parted like a respectful sea as Matt approached.

It didn't hit her until they reached the end of their totally silent journey that he hadn't once asked directions.

'How did you know where I live?' she asked as he came around to open the passenger door for her—there was hardly any trace of his limp now. 'Or where I'm working, for that matter…?'

'I made it my business to know.'

His matter-of-fact reply jolted her. 'That's outrageous!' she accused with shaky contempt.

'What was I supposed to do? Let you walk out of my life?'

The anger in his eyes confused Kat. Wasn't that exactly what he had done? It had certainly felt like it.

'I'm afraid I'm hopelessly out of date about such things. What does that involve, exactly…? Do you require the services of a private investigator or do you just punch a name up on a computer screen?'

'Depends on how much you need to know.'

Matt didn't tell her of the nights he'd stood outside himself, in the shadows, thinking about coming up and knocking on her door. A police patrol car had even stopped once and demanded to know his intentions.

Kat threw him a disgusted glance and slid the key into the rusty lock; the peeling front door opened. She didn't waste any time on social niceties, she got straight to the point.

'I expect you want to know if I co-operated with those magazine people?' Matt's enigmatic expression remained exasperatingly mysterious. 'That is why you're here, isn't it?' Still no joy. 'They did ring me once...' she conceded.

'That would figure.'

Perhaps his surveillance had already revealed this. The nonsensical notion of some grey-faced little man dutifully recording all her conversations brought a quiver of hysteria to her voice—he'd probably died of sheer boredom!

'But I didn't say a word, *honestly*...'

Matt didn't reply straight off; he was looking around her tiny bedsit in a horrified way that made her even more conscious of its extreme grottiness. It was clean—that was about the only nice thing that could be said of the spartan, threadbare conditions—but if she wanted to clear her debts this side of the next millennium she needed to keep her personal expenses to a minimum.

'It's very convenient for the hospital,' she chirped defensively.

Matt nodded noncommittally. He was feeling physically ill to think she'd been living in these sort of conditions for a whole month.

'Wait until she's calmed down,' his mother had counselled, and like an idiot for once in his life he'd listened!

'You didn't trust her.'

'Why didn't she tell me?'

'I expect she tried, but I don't suppose you were in a mood to listen. You learn the truth about her mother and you go running there wanting to make up—she'll spit in your eye,' his own mother had announced with convincing confidence. *'I would,'* she'd added frankly.

What had a month got him? The poor darling must hate his guts after seeing her face and a whole lot more plastered all over that damned rag. He could have co-operated and given them their damned story, but, *no* he'd had to put their backs up and virtually challenge them to write what the hell they liked about him... That invitation hadn't included a carte blanche on those he loved.

'I know you didn't give them the story...'

He watched her give a sigh of relief, as though she'd expected him to sail in here and blast her. But then why wouldn't she? he thought with a grimace of self-disgust, after the last time.

He cringed inside every time he thought about the things he'd said to her. She probably hates me!

'As for the picture...' Matt couldn't visualise that picture without wanting to smash something. He was fair game, but not Kathleen. 'I had no idea at all...'

'How could you?' Kat was too jumpy to notice the intensity of his tone. This was a very small room and Matt's larger-than-life vitality and sheer in-your-face sex appeal seemed to fill it. It was becoming an uphill battle to control her emotions. Throwing herself at his feet would be a crowning glory for what had been the most humiliating day of her life. She tried to look anywhere but at him...Matt wasn't an easy man not to notice.

'I've spoken to my lawyers,' he told her stiffly, 'and though it would give me the greatest pleasure to watch those swines choke on their telephoto lens in public—' his voice deepened, roughened '—the general consensus seems to be that a court case would only attract even more unwanted attention.'

Kat nodded her acceptance. 'It's good of you to come and tell me in person.'

Matt winced. 'I suppose I deserve that.'

Kat stared up at him in total incomprehension. 'Would you like a cup of tea?' she heard herself ask stupidly.

His powerful chest heaved. 'You're in shock.'

'I am?'

'You can't stay here,' he announced abruptly. His mobile

lips firmed into an obstinate line as he gave a decisive nod. 'Pack what you need for the night.'

'What are you talking about?' she flared in panic. Wasn't it enough she was driven to distraction by his presence? Did he have to act as if they were still a couple, just to add to her misery? 'It might not be up to your standards, but I live here.'

'Not any more, you don't.'

Startled, Kat forgot her intention of not looking at him and shot a sneaky peek at his face.

'If you can't stand the idea of moving in with me, you can stay with my mother…or a hotel, if you prefer, until we can organise something more suitable. I've ruined your reputation…' His expression grew even more taut and remote. 'Exposed you to the insults of sleazes like that creep in the car park.' The maverick nerve in his lean cheek began to jump. 'It's my responsibility to make things right!'

Kat's scrutiny stopped being furtive; her eyes widened. It was slowly dawning on her that, far from coming here to blame her for the article, Matt had placed her in the role of victim! The only person he seemed to be condemning was himself.

'Do women have reputations to ruin these days…?'

'Don't be flippant, Kathleen,' he reprimanded heavily.

'I find it hard to be serious,' she cried, 'when you're talking a load of sexist rubbish. If I go into hiding, which seems to be what you're suggesting, won't people assume I've done something to be ashamed of?'

Matt stilled. 'I'm glad you're not ashamed. Personally, I treasure the memory.'

'Me too,' she responded without thinking. With a gasp of dismay she pressed her hand to her lips; she couldn't bring herself to look at him. 'Anyhow, why should I need protecting any more than you do?'

'Don't be naïve,' he grated impatiently.

Kat glanced up. 'I'm not!'

'I'm used to seeing my life, or a dramatised version of it, in the tabloids. We both know that even in these enlightened times double standards are alive and well.'

Kat's eyes slid evasively away from the cynicism in his deep-set eyes. 'Even if what you say is true, how exactly are you going make things right?'

He opened a drawer and began extracting several items—all undergarments, as it happened. An equally agitated Kat immediately tried to shove them back in. With an exasperated growl Matt grabbed her wrist. His cerulean eyes raked her flushed face.

'I'm going to marry you, of course.'

Kat's nerveless fingers opened and the pretty pink bra she was grasping drifted to the floor. Her eyes followed the fluttering object till it fell in a heap at his feet. Slowly she lifted her head; it felt strangely heavy for her neck. Bosom heaving emotionally, she levelled her resentful eyes at him.

'Of course!' she echoed hoarsely. It was the *of course* part that got to her in a big way and made his casual announcement the final insult. Perhaps he thought because she'd offered him unquestioning obedience in bed she would do the same now! The angry thought opened the door and the forbidden erotic images came flooding into her head.

She tore her eyes from the stern outline of his sexy mouth. 'It's not as if I have any say in the matter!' Her voice rose shrilly. 'Don't you think that solution is a little...how can I put this?...*dramatic?*' she drawled scornfully.

Every fibre of her screamed rejection at the idea of Matt marrying her out of a misplaced sense of guilt. Was she meant to be grateful he was offering her the consolation prize? She wanted Matt, there was little point pretending otherwise, but she didn't want him on those terms. Duty was a pretty poor substitute for love. If he had really loved her he wouldn't have waited until now.

'You didn't always think it was such an amusing idea,' he reminded her softly.

'I'm not amused,' she bit back.

His firm jaw tightened. He was having the hardest time controlling his anger and an even harder time controlling his lust.

'Think about it, Kathleen. It makes sense.'

'Only to you!' she snapped. 'How long is this marriage supposed to last? Until my good name is re-established? I hardly think you've thought this through. I'm not some pathetic little woman who can't stand a bit of gossip, Matt! I plan on travelling...' So far her plans had only got as far as tentative enquiries, but she saw no point telling him this.

'Since when?'

His belligerent tone struck Kat as pretty damned perverse. Was she supposed to ask his permission? That was pretty rich coming from someone who hadn't even tried to contact her...or maybe this was someone talking who had *made it his business* to know where she was living and working? Perhaps he was annoyed his surveillance hadn't come up with this information.

'Since I decided that's what I want to do,' she explained sweetly. 'That's the joy of being a free agent,' she enthused... *Sure, I'm having a hell of time!* 'I hardly think my notoriety is going to follow me all the way there!'

Matt gave a cranky grunt that in less fraught circumstances might have made Kat laugh.

'Where is there?'

'Australia,' she improvised wildly. Why not...? If you were going to do something, you might as well go the whole hog, and you couldn't get much further away.

Matt swore. 'When?'

'December.'

'That's four months away! What are you going to do until then?'

She stuck her chin out and smiled. 'I'm going to ignore the gossips.'

'Don't try coming the hard nut with me…' His voice softened; the tenderness shattered her veneer of practicality in one stroke.

'I know otherwise. Are you trying to tell me you didn't feel violated when you saw yourself plastered all over that rag?'

She couldn't have put it better herself.

He captured her chin firmly between the palms of his hands and tilted her face up to him. 'Look at me, Kathleen.'

Kat gulped back a sob and did as he bade. His touch gentle, he tucked a strand of shiny fair hair behind her ear. The touch of his fingers against her skin made Kat shiver; the mixture of fear and arousal made the butterflies in her belly run riot.

The electric blue eyes staring fixedly down into her face carried a message that made her heart thud against her ribs. No, this was pity, she told her hopeful heart sternly. If he'd still felt anything he'd have followed her once he'd discovered his mistake…and he must have done so by now. His next words confirmed this.

'I know, of course—about your mother.' He spoke abruptly and seemed to find it hard to maintain eye contact. He hesitated, and that in itself was enough to astonish Kat, then he closed his eyes and she watched him visibly fight for composure. 'I was a total bastard to you,' he said bluntly.

'No…no!' she heard herself instinctively protest, even though she'd called him far worse herself during those long nights when she'd lain awake racked with longing for him.

Kat felt the heat build in her pale cheeks. Matt looked fairly startled by her agitated response, and small wonder!

'Well, you were,' she countered in a calmer voice. 'But there were extenuating circumstances.'

'You think so? Let me tell you about those extenuating circumstances,' he ground out harshly.

Eyes distant, she saw him look at the soft piece of pastel silk in his hand; he raised it to his face and inhaled deeply.

The careless action was made even more erotic for Kat by the fact it was totally unstudied—he seemed hardly aware of what he'd done. The rush of desire that flooded through her was so intense her body temperature soared several degrees in a single heartbeat—she was melting. If he'd chosen that moment to propose once again she'd have screamed yes and to hell with the consequences!

'In the early days I was the ideas man,' Matt was saying in a driven voice. Kat had to shake her head to clear the lust-induced fog. 'I had the contacts and I used them. I networked for all I was worth while Damon dealt with the day to day minutiae.'

'The money?' Kat suggested quietly.

'The money,' he agreed heavily. 'I was a fool!'

'You were a friend!' she protested.

'Listen up and you just might change your mind. When it finally came out that Damon had almost gambled the company away from underneath us, we had this almighty row.'

That didn't seem unreasonable to Kat, but it obviously held some major significance for Matt. His jaw clenched to breaking point as his eyes sought hers. The expression in those sombre depths sent a shiver of raw fear down her spine. She wasn't even aware that her hands had begun transcribing sweeping soothing motions over his strongly muscled upper arms.

'He went away and killed himself, Kathleen. He committed suicide.'

Kat's fractured sigh filled the silence that followed this starkly shocking announcement.

'That's terrible, Matt, but it's not your fault.'

'No? He was one of my best friends and I didn't help

him. All I could rant on about was the trust he'd betrayed, the jobs he'd lost... It was all me...me...! He needed help and I wasn't there. I thought, What if I couldn't be there for you? You'd be better off without me.'

The tears that had formed in her eyes began to run unchecked down her cheeks.

'*Never!*' she choked. Her tears weren't the only thing Kat couldn't check any longer; her feelings were flying out of control too.

Matt froze. As she watched the colour seeped slowly from his darkly toned skin. His hands slid up to her shoulders.

'*What did you say?*' he demanded in a strained, hollow voice that sounded totally unlike the Matt she knew...the Matt she loved... It didn't matter; she still loved this Matt—the one who had doubts and fears like everyone else, the one who looked as if he'd been to hell and back! Kat ached to soothe those frown lines from his forehead.

'I said I'd never be better off without you.' She felt his fingers tighten to grating point against her delicate collarbone.

'And that would be because...?' he prompted, with barely concealed impatience.

'Because I love you, probably.' She tilted her head to one side and seemed to consider the matter. 'Yes, that must be it....'

She didn't finish her sentence before, with a deep groan, his lips came crashing down on hers. The kiss was rough, raw and needy; it left her a blissful trembling wreck. Matt was trembling too.

'I love you so much,' he rasped, nuzzling deliciously at the delicate flesh around her ear. The nuzzling part was sending the pleasure zone in her brain delirious; the word part was doing some serious damage!

She took his beloved face between her hands. 'Why the hell didn't you say so straight off,' she demanded, 'instead of doing daft things like...?'

An amused light shone in Matt's eyes; he still felt kind of dizzy with sheer relief. He was never, *ever* going to listen to a single thing his mother told him again.

'Like propose…?' he teased throatily.

Kat gave a snort of disgust and gently bit the tip of his nose. *'To save my good name!'*

'Well, I was desperate,' he offered in defence.

Kat grinned extremely smugly. 'You were?'

'I've never known anyone like you, Kathleen.'

'I was under the impression,' she retorted drily, 'you've *known* lots of women.'

'Sure, but, like me, they were selfish as hell. I discovered early on that it's easier to give *things* than part of yourself. Then you came along.' He gazed at her with unconcealed wonder. 'You blew me away! I've never had anyone give without asking anything in return, and you, my love, gave me your innocence, your trust, your heart!' His expression darkened. 'And what did I do with them…?'

'Don't, Matt,' she pleaded, unable to stand the self-loathing in his eyes.

'The past month has been pure unadulterated hell. I wanted to come to you but I was sure you'd spit in my eye, to quote someone we both know.'

'Drusilla…?'

He nodded.

Kat could see the shadow of that hell he spoke so eloquently of in his eyes, so she decided to kiss it away. She was quite successful, and it took some time to do the job properly. When she finally paused to check how much progress she had made, they were both lying full length on her rickety two-seater sofa; a lot of Matt's long legs were over the arm and her head was against his shoulder.

'I've just had the most marvellous idea! About Joe,' she explained, snuggling up to him.

'I'm not sure I like you thinking about Joe when I'm kissing you.'

'You're not kissing me,' she pointed out reasonably.

'That can soon be fixed.'

Laughing huskily, Kat evaded his lustful advances. 'Joe and Emma. Wouldn't it be marvellous if—?'

Matt groaned. 'No, definitely not!' he said firmly. 'In fact, I'm only going to marry you on the condition you hang up your matchmaker hat for good.'

Kat pouted prettily and gave a little sigh.

'Well, in that case...' With a sinuous little wriggle she flipped herself over onto her tummy. Her fingers strayed over the crisp dark whorls of dark hair on his chest. 'You're a wet blanket, but I don't suppose I have much choice—if you love me, that is. You *do* love me?'

'It might take the next fifty years, but I think I should be able to prove it to you eventually.'

Kat eyes widened in mock alarm. 'Fifty years? I was thinking of something a bit more immediate.' She shot him a wicked little look from under the sweep of her lashes. 'If you get my drift,' she explained innocently as her nimble fingers slid under his belt.

Matt gasped and then grinned; she was happy to see his ego had made a full recovery. 'How much proof do you need?' he wondered, slipping the front fastening catch on her bra. 'Ah!' he sighed as her soft white flesh spilled out

'Quite a lot,' she whispered throatily.

'That shouldn't be a problem.'

'You're very confident,' she teased, leaning forward so the tips of her breasts rubbed provocatively against his bare chest.

His eyes darkened; his fingers wove into her loose silky tresses and he pulled her face down to him. 'I'll let you be the judge of whether that confidence is justified or not,' he rasped.

Kat knew her decision was a foregone conclusion.

*   *   *

'There he is! There he is!' Joe yelled beside her, but Kat had already seen the tall figure running towards the finish line amongst a group of serious club runners.

The fun runners, with their hilarious, often highly uncomfortable costumes, would arrive much later. These fit specimens were all similarly clad in running vests and shorts, but for Kat's money there was only one pair of legs worth looking at!

Glancing down at the tiny figure asleep in the padded papoose sling nestled against her bosom, she wove her way between the crowds around the finish line, ultra-protective of her burden.

Matt was bent over his hands clamped against his thighs, breathing hard. He lifted his head as someone breathlessly called across congratulations.

'Just a gentle jog...?'

He straightened up, a grin on his face when he heard the gently sarcastic gibe.

Close to, she could see his bronzed body gleamed with a healthy sweat, but otherwise he looked remarkably unaffected by the ordeal he'd just inflicted on himself. Kat was relieved; despite the fact he'd obeyed her strictures about a sensible training regime, she had had some reservations about him attempting the London Marathon so soon after his accident. Kat had never had any doubts that he'd finish; it had just been a matter of when, and in what condition!

'Pretty good time...huh...?'

He sounded almost as proud as the first time he'd held their baby daughter and spoken her name. Kat watched with loving affection as he greedily swigged back a bottle of water.

A young woman came forward, bearing a shiny reflective body wrap to help him retain his body heat; with a nod Kat took it from her. She draped it carefully around her husband's broad shoulders.

'It didn't give you any problems?' she asked.

Matt shucked the foil wrap over his shoulders and slapped the side of his left leg. 'None at all.' His blue eyes darkened as they came to rest on his wife's face. 'You know, angel, when I promised myself, that day they told me I might never walk again, that some day I'd run the Marathon, part of me thought I might be doing it in a wheelchair.'

Kat's eyes filled with tears. 'I know.'

A grin banished the solemnity from his face. 'One scenario I never, *ever* imagined was having the two most important women in my life waiting for me at the finish line.'

The unconditional love shining in his eyes brought a solid lump of emotion to Kat's throat. She rubbed her cheek against his shoulder as he moved closer and lifted the corner of the tiny bonnet that covered their daughter's downy head.

'How has she been?' he whispered.

'A bit fretful earlier, but she's settled now.'

Kat understood his concern. They were both still a little over-protective of their baby who, had she been born at full term, would now only be a couple of weeks old; as it was nearly three months had elapsed since Kat had given birth Little Anna had spent the first ten weeks of her life in special care.

During those traumatic weeks, when things had sometimes looked pretty bleak, Kat had grown to appreciate perhaps for the first time the strength of this man she'd married. She knew that without his love and unfailing support she couldn't have survived that ordeal.

'All we have to do now is make the sponsors pay up.'

Matt was wearing the logos of two charities very close to their hearts: one concerned with spinal injuries and the other a support group for parents of premature babies.

'Leave that to me.'

'Don't I always?' His pride was obvious as he looked

down at his beautiful wife. 'Do I get a kiss, or do you want to wait until I've had a shower?'

Smiling, Kat raised herself on tiptoes, one arm protectively across her chest and the sleeping baby. 'Since when,' she whispered in his ear, 'did I have a problem with you being hot and sticky...?'

With a husky laugh he drank from her lips with even more eagerness than he'd displayed for the water bottle.

'The next time we'll have to do it together,' he reflected thoughtfully.

'I thought we did.'

With a grin Matt patted her behind. 'Not *that* it, the Marathon it.'

'Me?'

Matt laughed at the horrified expression on her face. 'You'll love it.'

'Definitely not!' she said firmly.

'We'll see...'

Kat sighed. She knew he'd talk her round; he always did. Maybe it wouldn't be so bad... She looked from her big, bold, media-shy husband, who was skilfully selling his chosen charities to a TV film crew who had recognised him, to their baby daughter and she felt a rush of pride; they were a team!

She had years of doing crazy things with Matt to look forward to. Was it any wonder she felt happy enough to burst?

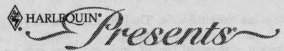

If you enjoyed what you just read,
then we've got an offer you can't resist!

Take 2 bestselling
love stories FREE!

Plus get a FREE surprise gift!

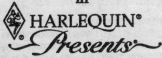

Three of romance's most talented craftsmen
come together in one special collection.

New York Times bestselling authors

Jayne Ann Krentz

Tess Gerritsen

National bestselling author

Stella Cameron

in

Stolen Memories

With plenty of page-turning passion and dramatic
storytelling, this volume promises many memorable
hours of reading enjoyment!

Coming to your favorite retail outlet in February 2002.

HARLEQUIN®

Makes any time special ®

Visit us at www.eHarlequin.com

PHSM-MMP

Coming Next Month

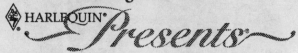

THE BEST HAS JUST GOTTEN BETTER!

HPCNM0202R